By David Delman

SUDDEN DEATH
A WEEK TO KILL
A TIME TO MARRY
THE HARD SELL

SUDDEN DEATH

SUDDEN DEATH

DAVID DELMAN

PUBLISHED FOR THE CRIME CLUB BY
DOUBLEDAY & COMPANY, INC.,
GARDEN CITY, NEW YORK
1972

Printed in the United States of America

For my children:
Betsy, Jane, and Nancy.
With all my love.

CONTENTS

AUTHOR'S NOTE

As I write this, peace—or at least a workable truce—seems ready to calm the factionalism that has troubled organized tennis. Thus, by setting my novel in the near but otherwise unspecified future, I felt free to gloss over that particular brand of strife. As for my choice of tie-breaker, I know that Sudden Death finds more adherents among fans than among players. Still, I like it very much indeed for its nail-biting drama. And since it is my book . . .

SUDDEN DEATH

CHAPTER 1

BEFORE THE FACT

It was a wicked cross-court backhand, hit with top spin, hit with Cole leaning the wrong way, hit beyond his reach. It should have left him dead. It didn't. He launched himself at it and got a piece of it with the frame of his racket a split second before that goddam racket went flying from his hand. The ball danced on the tape, then dropped. To my side of the net. *I* was dead.

The Merion gallery exploded, the kind of visceral reaction you get only once in a while from a tennis crowd. In a more detached moment, I wouldn't have blamed them. It had been a tremendous effort. As it was, I hated them. And I hated Cole, too, though that was nothing new.

Grinning, he got to his feet. He shook his long hair out of his eyes, making a thing of it for the gallery. Then, slowly, he went to retrieve his racket from the doubles alley. I watched all this unmoving, nailed to the grass by disbelief. Racket in hand, he came back toward the net. Still grinning, he bent toward me.

"Now, I'm gonna whip your tail," he said softly.

And, of course, he did.

He went on to break my service, making the game score six-all and moving us into the tie-breaker, a nine-point Sudden Death. The red flag went up to so inform the gallery. Normally, Sudden Death time is a time of tension. It can be almost eerie with hush and expectancy. Seat edges only. On this day, false alarm. Because the nine-point Sudden Death ended in five, which is like expecting a crash and getting a whimper. He served the first two points, I served the next two, and then his *coup de grâce* to my backhand completed the blitz. It also evened the match at a set apiece. It also snapped a racket string. I eyed it as if it were Benedict Arnold.

For the next two sets, he did to me exactly as he'd promised. It was savage, brutalizing tennis. He lobbed me when he wanted to, chopped me when he wanted to, and hammered me into submission in between. There was nothing I could do about it. It was Cole Cooper playing the kind of tennis perhaps only half a dozen men in the history of the sport had ever been capable of, and me playing exactly the kind of tennis I'd played most of the year, which is to say terrible. And as he ravaged me, as the points piled up on his side like chips in a nightmarish poker game, I thought, bitterly, of the eight years between his twenty-six and my thirty-four. And of how much sadistic pleasure he took in inflicting this kind of humiliation. And of how much I wanted to get at him with my hands.

And then finally he smashed a desperation lob of mine to the base line for an easy winner, and it was over. As polite applause rustled through the gallery, I realized, suddenly, that it had been strangely silent over the past several minutes. They, the buffs, hadn't liked it either. That wouldn't bother Cole, I knew. Still, it was a little something for me to take away.

He leaped the net. Nobody does that anymore, but he did. "Why don't you quit, old-timer," he said, smiling, his paw extended as if he really thought I might take it.

"Why don't you die?" I said.

In the locker room I found Berto and Chris Hazlett waiting for me. Berto, seeing my face, kept his expressionless. He'd known me for seventeen years—my roommate in college, my doubles partner all over the world—and he understood things like when he should and shouldn't show sympathy. Chris didn't. Chris had been Cole's whipping boy at Wimbledon the month before, and in my humiliation he'd watched a rerun of his own. And besides he'd been drinking. He said, "Three years ago, two years ago, you would've killed the ruddy bloke."

I said, "Shut your goddam face."

He blinked.

I added, "Haul out of here, you drunken sot, and ship yourself back to Melbourne."

So Berto moved between us. Putting his hands on my shoulders, he forced me to sit on the bench. After that, he came around behind and began doing serviceable things to the knotted muscles in my back. "Beg the man's pardon," he said.

I said nothing, while Chris peered at me anxiously.

"Matty," Berto said, "beg the man's pardon."

I let my breath out heavily. "Yeah," I said. "I'm sorry, Chris."

He smiled in relief, and Berto said, "With age comes wisdom. Three years ago, two years ago, you would have died on the rack before you did anything as civilized as acknowledge error. Berto is pleased at all signs of human development."

"Berto talks too much," I said. "Berto always has." But I felt better now, and in a moment I stood up and started for the showers. Then Cole came in. Behind him, Wally Edmiston (as always) carrying Cole's rackets as if they were royal. Wally didn't play tournament tennis anymore. Wally had one eye. He'd lost the other on a narrow, curve-infested mountain road in France two years ago because the Citroën he was in was being driven too idiotically fast for such a mountain road. And who'd been pushing this Citroën? Cole. Yes, Cole.

3

In Wally, was there a residue of rancor toward the man whose carelessness had cost him a useful eye and a promising career? If there was, it was a mote so negligible as to be visible only through high magnification. He was Cole's faithful retainer, his serf. And it was not pleasant to see one man in such eager thralldom to another, particularly when devotion went so ill rewarded.

Cole's Southern accent was adjustable—thickest when he most wanted to provoke. "It's a wake, I do declare," he said. "Wally, look at these li'l ol' boys. . . . I mean really check 'em out so as you can tell me which one's the stiff."

To this, all of us reacted in our characteristic fashions. Wally laughed, on cue. I snarled something under my breath and resumed my interrupted progress toward the showers. Berto arranged his grandee's features in a Spanish death mask. But Chris, as Cole well knew, was eminently goadable—a condition not foreign to a man who is on his way down and senses it.

Fair skin fiery at the cheekbones, he said, "You're such a lucky blighter, Cooper. When I was in my prime—"

"That's the one," Cole said. "That's the stiff. By God, a voice from the grave, sure enough."

I stopped. "Leave him alone," I said.

"Why?"

"What's the matter with you anyway? Even for you, you're being disgusting."

"I can fight my own ruddy battles," Chris said, his hands clenching into fists. He was five-eight and a puffy one hundred and sixty. Like me, Cole was six-one and just under two hundred. Long white-gold hair, full beard, ice blue eyes to match his smile—the smile of a Viking at a Saxon blood bath—he stood there looking arrogant and absolutely merciless. And, by contrast, he brought Chris's small potbelly into bold relief. It was an ugly mismatch.

"Berto," I said warningly.

4

He nodded. He put his hands on Chris's shoulders and made soothing sounds to him, while ushering him toward an exit. It wasn't easy—liquor and temper were blurring Chris's sense of survival—but Berto had his ways.

Surprisingly, Cole kept his mouth shut during this operation, and as long as he did, so did Wally. With Berto and Chris gone, I headed once more for the showers. A few minutes later I was joined there by Cole.

"Where's Wally? I mean doesn't he come in to soap your back?"

He grinned. "He wanted to, but I sent him away. Wouldn't do to spoil him."

"Of course not."

"Wally digs me. Ever since we were li'l ol' boys in Richmond, Wally's had this thing for me. And you know, I try to be kind, but there are limits, right?"

I kept silent.

"Wouldn't you say I try to be kind, Matty?"

"Like a rattler is kind."

He threw back his head and acted out how much this amused him. "You *don't* dig me, Matty. You sure enough don't. You been writing letters to me?"

"Letters?"

He wasn't laughing now. He was studying me hard, and all of a sudden it struck me that something really was bugging him. I mean usually Cole was unspeakable without trying, but on this day he'd been trying. I liked the idea of something bugging Cole. Liked it so much I stopped soaping so I could watch him as carefully as he'd been watching me.

"Somebody been writing you letters?" I asked. "What kind of letters?"

"My pappy used to say to me—Cole, boy, when you grow up hardest thing in the world will be to spot when a man's truth-telling."

5

"What kind of letters, Cole?"

He turned off his shower and went back into the locker room. I followed two steps behind him. "Threatening letters, Cole?"

He didn't answer. I could tell I was irritating him a little, and this was a brand-new and exhilarating experience for me. A reversal of roles—me getting under Cole's skin. It felt marvelous. "Somebody scaring you, Cole?"

"That'll be the day, sure enough."

"But maybe you *ought* to be scared. A lot of people don't like you, how's that for a piece of news? I mean one or two of those people you've been rotten to actually resent it."

"Gutless wonders."

"All of them?"

"All of them, including you."

"Sure enough?"

And glory be, now he was angry in a way I'd never seen before. "You think I give a hoot and a holler what you think of me . . . what anybody thinks of me? Not one tinker's damn, ol' buddy. The world is made up of two kinds of people— those who gets and those who don't."

"I like that, Cole. That's profound. Is that another goody your old pappy taught you?"

"My old pappy lived to be eighty-one—"

"They all do. It's the thing about old pappys."

"Eighty-one years old, and he never had but one good day, the day he died. All those years of working his butt off, scrabbing at the soil to keep body and soul together. That's my old pappy. But it sure enough ain't his son. No, sir. Maybe it'll be a short life . . . who gives a damn, so long as there's lots of lovin' and lots of gold."

"A short life, Cole?"

"Go to hell."

"Is that what those letters are all about? Is some public-spirited citizen threatening you? Come on, let me see them."

"Go to hell."

"Now wait a minute. Maybe I have been writing them, but I've blocked out, see, and looking at them again will bring it all back."

"Either you or Berto," he said.

"Why Berto?"

"Because it's exactly what that Puerto Rican hot dog would think is funny."

About that he was right. Berto had that failing. It suited his special dichotomy, part aristocrat, part clown. And a practical joke that could torment Cole, even a little, would provide Berto with the most extreme kind of satisfaction. The fact was I, too, saw Berto's hand in this. Still, there was no point in letting Cole off the hook by acknowledging that. No point at all.

"But there's all kinds of people who find you less than lovable," I said. "I mean if I were you I wouldn't just willy-nilly assume it's a joke. I mean there's Chris, for instance. And, in addition to Berto and me, there's Timmy Clark—"

"Uppity Nigra," he muttered.

"Nigra?"

"Shouldn't be allowed on a court with a white man."

"Yes, he's heard you say that. It endears you to him."

He shrugged. "There's good woollyheads and bad woolly-heads. He's a bad one, but just a woollyhead and no more than that. You trying to tell me he's worth worrying about?"

"That's right. That's what I'm trying to tell you. He hates your insides."

"Lots of them do that. But back where I come from they still get themselves off the street to let me pass by."

"Sure enough?"

"You heard me."

"Timmy does?"

He didn't answer.

"Speak up, Cole."

"He's always had Elinore and her daddy protecting him. So he gets away with stuff."

"Good heavens, I almost left Elinore off my list. Does your wife still find you lovable?"

"Man, man, that woman will find me lovable till the day she dies."

"Even though you walked out on her?"

"I could beat her bloody, and it wouldn't change a thing. She'd kiss the hand that blacked her eyes if I asked her to. You know that."

And I did. And because I did, suddenly the fun went out of it for me. "She's too damned good for you," I said sourly.

I was finished dressing now and started out of the locker room, almost bumping into Wally, who had apparently been standing in the doorway for some time, listening. "Why don't you grow up?" I said angrily. "You've got better things to do with your life than be at that bastard's beck and call."

"He's my friend, Matty."

"He's not your friend. You're his thing. Why the hell can't you see that?"

"Hey, Matty," Cole said.

I turned.

"Does *she* still find me lovable?"

"Who?"

"*Your* wife."

Reflexively, I took a step toward him, but then Wally, his voice almost apologetic, said, "It'd be two against one, Matty."

Some agent. Would you believe Wally Edmiston was *my* agent? Not Cole's, mine. It was a wrench, but I left them. Three years ago, two years ago I would not have. Berto would have been pleased at still another sign of human development.

My intention had been to return to the gallery to join Berto and Chris there as spectators. Timmy Clark was in the second semi-final—the first semi-final, in case I haven't made it plain, was that monstrosity featuring me. Timmy was up against Jess Cavendish, a big Australian kid who'd given me fits at Wimbledon before unraveling and handing me the match on errors. So, with the U. S. Open just around the corner, both players were of more than passing interest to me. Timmy, in particular. He'd had a fine year and would probably go into the tournament seeded second behind Cole. And there were those, Berto among them, who felt that stroke for stroke—that is, intangibles such as temperament aside—Timmy was second to nobody in the world. Only you couldn't set temperament aside. And Timmy's was super-heated where Cole was concerned. It's hard to hate a man as much as Timmy hated Cole and play sound tennis against him. It really is. Tennis is a game of intense concentration . . . of seeing your opponent clearly enough to exploit all weaknesses. But a murderous haze is a hard thing to see through clearly. I know. Peering through one, I headed for the parking lot instead of Cavendish versus Clark. I found Berto's car. I sat in it. Ten minutes later I felt a little less primordial.

But that final barb Cole had tossed so accurately was still stuck in my throat, causing me all manner of discomfort. The thing is I'd begun to believe I might be getting over Meg. It had been three years since she'd stopped being my wife and almost that long since I'd seen her last. Recently, I'd even managed to put four or five days back to back without having to evict her forcibly from my mind. Four or five days? Not impressively long, you say. Not enough, you say, to encourage a man in the belief that he was safely on the far side. Well, maybe not. Except that I'd never been able to do that before. An isolated day here and there, yes—but not a skein of four or five. *That* had been encouraging. Also illusory, as Cole had demonstrated. One thing you could always give Cole credit for, how adept he was at shattering illusions.

So I stayed on there in Berto's car, in seclusion, because when you have to think about rotten things . . . when you have no choice but to think about things as rotten as Meg and Cole . . . you don't want it to be in public. You don't want people watching you. It's the wounded-animal syndrome.

Meg. Let me tell you a little about Meg Fraser. She's twenty-seven now, but I can only describe her to you the way she looked when she was still Meg Fraser Mathews. If I had introduced her to you then, say three years ago, you would have seen a small gray-eyed blonde. Generous mouth, short, straight nose, a dusting of freckles on the bridge. Hair worn short and in bangs. *Dark* blond hair, very fine, so fine that the last breeze could shift the pattern of its fall, causing subtle shifts in her expression. A smile, for instance, could remain a smile, but be a different smile. Same lip formation, same muscle control, and yet a smile to say something other than it had an instant ago. Now that's mysterious. A small girl, yes; delicately boned, but deep-breasted. With a pair of legs to break a man's heart.

Meg was an only child. Unlike mine, her parents were loaded. We were both Angelenos, but while I learned my tennis on public courts, she learned hers at country clubs. That's another way of saying her father was a big-deal corporation lawyer while mine was a small-time insurance salesman. I met Meg at Wimbledon when I was as old as she is now, seven years ago. I saw her mowed down by Dot Magruder in the quarter-finals. She fought so hard, looked so pretty, and was so hopelessly outclassed I think I fell instantly in love with her. I was waiting for her when she came out of the dressing room. She knew who I was. That year, everybody knew who I was. It was my great year—an eyelash short of the grand slam: the French and Australian championships, Wimbledon, and then that squeaker of a loss to Berto in the finals at Forest Hills.

"She's too big and strong," Meg said. "It wasn't fair."

"No."

"I battled though, didn't I?"

"You sure did."

"Are you waiting for me?"

"Yes."

"Why? Because you want to do something nice like take me for a drive through the pretty English countryside so I can think of something besides tennis?"

"I had that in mind."

She took my arm, and it's hard to convey how pleased I was by the sweetness of that simple gesture. Five months later—over the energetic objections of her parents, and the apathy of mine—we were married. It was wonderful for the first three years. It was awful after that. My fault more than hers, and the kind of blame that attaches to her involves things she couldn't much help. Like being too young, too unprepared for coping with someone as hagridden as I was —the hag being tennis, of course.

She used to say to me, "I like to win, too—but if you lose, you lose, so what? Why isn't it enough to be marvelous at what you do? Why do you have to be the absolute best at it?" And I could never explain it to her satisfactorily—mostly because I never understood it well enough myself, except in glib, parlor-psychiatry terms. I mean in terms of my father being a loser and me not wanting to be like him. But when you say that to a woman who happens to be crying bitterly at the time, you really haven't said a lot that's useful.

Once, when we were fighting, she described me to myself on the tennis court. She said my habitual expression was a deep and hostile scowl, a fanatic's scowl, as if my opponents were all prisoners in the dock, and I their hanging judge. I told her she was wrong. I told her it was never my opponents I hated but losing. She said it wasn't much of a distinction, and I think now she was right.

For my part, I didn't understand how much resentment and jealousy were building in her, how much she had come to regard tennis—rightly, of course—as Jezebel, her rival. Not even when she stopped playing, not even when she stopped coming to see me play. Predictably, I suppose, the breakup finally happened when I was in the middle of an appalling slump. My game had turned suddenly, inexplicably sour. Why? I don't know. Who ever knows about slumps. Overtennised, maybe. Too many tournaments, too much traveling. A staleness of body and mind. Thank God, it's never happened quite like that since. I mean this hasn't been a good year for me, but it's nothing like the horror that one was. Small boys were beating me. High school hotshots were spotting me two games per set. Berto said my tennis was like his toothless old uncle—gummy and unproductive, and it was the year Cole Cooper beat me for the first time after eighteen fruitless months of trying. Belaboring the obvious, I tell you I was not fit to live with.

So Meg chose not to. As I think you've gathered, I don't fault her for that. It was the raw and punishing way of it that sticks in my psyche. Wimbledon is where it happened. Seeded seventh, which was high considering the shabbiness of my year-long performance, I had failed to reach even the round of sixteen. Cole had attended to me, straight sets.

I should have taken Meg home then but didn't because Berto was still in the tournament. We'd always done that for each other, stayed around as long as one of us was in contention. Still, she wanted to leave, and I should have listened to the desperation in her voice. "I'm up to here with tennis and tennis players," she said. "Matty, I need to be with humans again. And so do you, whether you know it or not." Just a touch of insight would have been sufficient to show me how serious the need was. But insight was in short supply just then, though crud wasn't. I ranted about loyalty, about betrayal, about *her* insensitivity. The truth was that if she expressed a need to go, I felt it vital to stay. I mean this was axiomatic—as if, somehow, my manhood was at stake. That's what it had come to between us. When I say I was not fit to live with, I do not understate.

Cole beat Berto in a five-set final, and Elinore, Cole's bride of six months, announced a celebration. "You're jealous of him," Meg said when I told her I'd refused the invitation.

"Don't be ridiculous."

"Of course you are. Because he trimmed you, and because you can see it happening again."

"If I'm jealous, maybe I've got better reasons than that. I think you've been spending too much time with him."

"Go to hell."

"I see you off in goddam corners together."

"I'm going to Elinore's party," she said. "Either with you or without you."

So we went, and I very quickly, very intently got myself drunk. And time passed. And around midnight I began wandering through that huge house Elinore had rented for the tournament, looking for Meg. I found Elinore first. In front of the door to one of the second-floor bedrooms. I remember how white her face was. But her voice was quite steady. "Don't go in there," she said. "I just made that mistake."

I brushed her aside.

Meg was on the bed, face down. Cole sat on the edge of the bed, in shirt and trousers, putting on his shoes. I grabbed handfuls of his shirt, pulled him up, then knocked him down again. He lay there on the floor, laughing at me. He said, "I'd whip you good, ol' buddy, except I might hurt my tennis hand."

Meg didn't lift her head. "Look at me," I said, but she didn't turn. Elinore touched my arm. "You better go," she said softly. And so I did.

Well, you know what time does to anger. No matter how

much you want to keep it pure, time denatures it, adulterates it, so that you wake up one day with only an alloy. On another day, Cole speaks to you and before you know it you've answered him. And though you feel a stab of self-betrayal an instant later, there it is. Time and flux have done you in. At least that's the way it was with me. So where was time with Meg the case in point? I don't know. But it's easy to get paranoid about it. It's tempting to say time plays games with some of us—eroding what you want to keep, ignoring what it ought to dull.

Berto's voice: "Timmy in straight sets. Señor Cavendish is a comer, but he has learning to do. Timmy took his backhand apart. What happened to you?"

"A little tired, that's all."

He studied me for a moment. "Matty *doloroso*. You wish to talk about it, *compadre?*"

"No. Have you been writing threatening notes to Cole Cooper?"

"Berto?" he said, casting his eyebrows to the sky.

"You're a barefaced liar," I said.

CHAPTER 2

ELINORE ALLOWAY COOPER,
HER PAD

Elinore Alloway Cooper was very rich. Her daddy, they said, owned the half of Richmond, Virginia, he wanted. She was also one of the kindest, most instinctively generous people I knew. Please, any Freudians who might be reading this, I want nothing at all about guilt or over-compensation, none of that. Elinore was lovely. I want it left that way.

But plain to look at, so plain. She was too tall and thin. Liking her as much as I did, I examined her face from time to time, wondering if skill could make more of it. But her hair was hair, her eyes were eyes, and so it went. Mercilessly.

Elinore was separated, not divorced, from Cole. Though there had been many Meg-like incidents in the four years of their marriage, she refused to give him a divorce. Cole was famous for his incidents. Cooper, the Zeus of the touring pros; a stud of mythic proportions. That was the Cooper legend, and yet it was he who walked out. I mean she hadn't thrown him out. Thirty now, four years older than Cole, Elinore had married him, she said, because she thought she was pregnant. She hadn't been. And it has occurred to me that maybe she never really believed she was but used pregnancy as a convincer for Daddy. Daddy, who in his semi-detached way, doted on Elinore, was not overly fond of Cole. He had started out liking him but then got to know him better.

"Of course Cole's hurt me," Elinore said to me in a typical defense against an oft-mounted onslaught. "But isn't that a way of knowing you're alive? Before Cole I was a rich, carefully reared zombie. I was positively antiseptic. No one had ever touched me. I guess no one particularly wanted to. I looked forward to a life of causes, general good works, and probably a touch of religious mania before I died a cracked old lady. Then Cole made love to me, and suddenly I had flesh and blood like the rest of you. I want him back—on his terms, whatever they are."

But she was out of her class, I feared. Cole had what he wanted from her, her money. It was the fount of her charm for him. Ironic, right? Her money was the only effective weapon she had, but she wouldn't use it as such. She wouldn't withhold it from him. And Cole knew she wouldn't.

I mentioned that Elinore was kind. The Richmond Wreckers could report that in detail. The Richmond Wreckers was the sobriquet tennis reporters hung on Cole, Timmy, Ann, and Wally when they were juniors and beating hell out of all the sixteen-, seventeen-year-olds in sight. But the point is that Cole, Timmy, and Ann were strays, starvelings, waifs that Elinore took in out of the cold. (Not Wally. Wally's folks owned the other half of Richmond. I exaggerate. But the idea's there.) She fed them, clothed them, taught them about ladies and gents, and then, when they were ready, got Daddy to pay their way through William and Mary. It's a fascinating story. I got some of it from Elinore, some of it from Wally, some of it from Ann, some of it from Daddy, a smidgin of it from Timmy, none of it from Cole, and a lot of it, unavoidably, from feature stories and magazines. For a while the Richmond Wreckers were the hottest tennis copy going.

But it all began with Daddy. Daddy, a widower from the time Elinore was three, was a wheeler-dealer. That was part of it. The other part of it was he was a tennis nut. Good enough to win three games from Tilden in a set he described for me point by point the first time I was a weekend guest at Alloway Manor. Well, about fifteen years ago Daddy got excited about the idea that there might be an untapped mine of tennis talent buried somewhere in Richmond. Not the rich kids who were usually attracted to the game, but poor kids who under ordinary circumstances never would be. *Natural* tennis players. Like the eighteenth century idea of the natural genius. So he decided to make a project out of it, and that gets us back to Daddy, the wheeler-dealer. Because, according to Elinore, Daddy wheeled and dealed so fast from project to project that some of them got lost in the shuffle. Which is what happened here for a bit.

But while it was still aglow from him, Daddy let it be known he was prospecting for tennis talent. I don't mean he advertised. I mean he dropped a hint here and there, but that was all it took. Elinore says she never knew how many kids were brought to him for inspection, but one day she returned from the posh Pennsylvania school he'd sent her to, summer vacation, to find Cole, Timmy, and Ann aboard in her house like stowaways. And no Daddy. He was in Africa, prospecting, now, for diamonds. He spent six months prospecting for diamonds.

Wild. Elinore arrives home, expecting to find Daddy and finds three raggle-taggle kids instead—all around ten years old with no one to look after them but a group of not very interested servants. The only thing Daddy had arranged for them before taking off was daily tennis lessons. No clothes, no schooling, just the country club pro coming to the house every day.

I said three kids. Actually, there were four. Wally was already part of the group. Exactly how that came about, even Wally doesn't remember for sure. He knows it was through the tennis pro, but beyond that he can't say. Or he won't say. That's possible, too. You go along sucked into thinking of

Wally as uncomplicated to the point of simple-mindedness, but then he'll say or not say something to warn you there might be a murky, secretive side to him. At any rate the first time Elinore saw them as a group, Ann was sitting on Wally's head. This was to keep him from taking a role in the main action, which featured Timmy and Cole, locked in combat and rolling around that way on the front lawn. It wasn't that Ann was bigger or stronger than Wally. But she had a croquet mallet. And she'd told him she would use it to break his leg. And he'd believed her—as he always would. Incidentally, it wasn't either that Ann gave much of a damn about who won the wrestling match. But she had lots of energy. And sometimes she dealt herself in just for the sake of being active.

Elinore viewed this scene from Daddy's Rolls, which had carried her home from the airport. In fact the Cole-Timmy tandem had come perilously close to disappearing under its gorgeous wheel. The Rolls screeched to a stop. A moment later, a large black chauffeur named Duncan, extremely irritated, had the boys by their respective scruffs and was hauling them apart. As Elinore recalls it, the burst of dialogue this triggered went something like this:

COLE: Let go of me, woollyhead.

DUNCAN (To Elinore): What this boy needs? He needs his mouth washed out with soap.

TIMMY: Let go of him. Let him go. I'll kill him.

The reason Elinore remembered this so vividly was it set the tone for so much of the Cole-Timmy relationship. And yet not all of that relationship. Though neither of them was prone to admit it these days, there were peaceful, almost amicable stretches during their growing up. Not vast stretches, but they existed. In fact Wally once told me, bitterly enough, that if Timmy had been white he thought Cole would have preferred him above all others. "He'd have liked him better than me," he said. "I used to tell everybody

Cole and I were best friends, but it wasn't so. Never was. I know that. You think I don't, but I do. I mean even when we were kids, Cole let me hang around mostly because my parents had so much money, and he thought, even then, maybe that would be useful to him some day. Same with Ann. And my parents saw that, and didn't trust either of them, and tried to get me to keep away from them. But I couldn't. I mean sometimes I really hated Cole, but I couldn't stay away from him. Ann used to laugh at me and call me his shadow, but that didn't mean anything. He was like a magnet, you know? All he had to do was lift a finger, and you came to him. Not just me. Other people, too."

So Elinore exited the Rolls and entered parenthood. Their real parents? Well, Cole's pappy was *not* one of those magnetized by him. Five years passed before Elinore looked on the ancient husk that was Tracy Cooper. And then he didn't look back. He was in a box about to be buried—a funeral she dragged Cole to, kicking and screaming. Ann and Timmy were orphans. The orphanages they came out of did not miss them noticeably. Actually, the operators of these orphanages had engaged in transactions with Daddy involving substantial sums. Thus, they were careful, Elinore felt, to avoid Alloway Manor as they might a pest house. To them, no news was good news. They had no wish to encounter ethical dilemmas, which is to say anything that might make it necessary to reclaim the orphans and return the money.

It wasn't that Elinore *planned* to become a mother at the age of fourteen. It was just that things had to be done for her waifs, and over the course of that summer she did them. And then she kept on doing them. In part because the woods were not full of volunteers offering to relieve her of her burden. And in part because she was a born taker-up-of-slack.

"Now please don't think of Daddy as a man who would be deliberately cruel to children," she said to me. "He wouldn't be. If he'd stopped to think about what he was doıng . . . but that's the point, you see. He's a man who tends to become . . . well self-preoccupied puts as good a face on it as any. And, of course, what complicated everything was that thing between Cole and Timmy. I mean Daddy is color blind, but it was truly outrageous of him to ignore the possibility that Cole and Timmy might not be."

But the tennis did go beautifully, and by the time Daddy got back, the happy owner of two new diamond mines, those kids were whaling the daylights out of the ball. All three dedicated themselves to tennis as if it were a religion. Which, in a way, it was—in the sense that through it they were being saved. Young as they were they understood this, and, as Elinore said, it was not really surprising. Poverty breeds its special insights.

Wally, who had a year's head start on them, began by beating Timmy and Cole badly. In turn Cole, who had half a year's growth on Timmy, began by regularly beating him. But these inequities yielded to time, and when all three were ready for their first sanctioned tournaments they stood this way in relation to each other: Cole, a slight edge over both; Timmy, a similarly slight edge over Wally. Ann's problem was finding competition. The boys were too much for her, the Richmond girls an insufficiency. Yet that, too, was a matter of time. As a sixteen-year-old, Ann was unbeatable. In the world of eighteen-year-olds, she encountered a harsher reality. But there were compensations. Men took to looking at her lingeringly. Not that this was new . . . changed, rather. A hypoed intensity, a perceptible increase in goatishness. And, at eighteen, Ann's dedication to tennis became slightly *less* than religious.

Hearing Cole on the subject of "Nigra" players—and Wally, too,—I wondered, every so often, how Elinore had got them on the court with Timmy, during all those years of growing up. Wondered from both ends. Because tractable was not a word that came readily to mind for Timmy either.

"I was stern with them," she said simply. But her eyes flickered a little, as if confronted by a parade of vivid if not totally pleasant memories. And that made me wonder in a different direction. About Elinore herself, and whether or not *her* dedication would prove indefinitely sustainable. At any rate, Daddy came home to exult in being Pygmalion—at least for a while. And Elinore never did return to her posh school in Pennsylvania.

So, as I guided my car up the tree-lined driveway that led to her posh house on Long Island, I wondered anew. Despite her brave talk, did she regret, sometimes, not having gone back in a hell of a hurry. That house . . . much better say mansion . . . made you think of things like that. I mean she'd bought it for its easy access to Forest Hills, for Cole in other words. Now there it stood—set off by three acres of scrupulously tended lawn and foliage. It was huge, majestic; chaste white columns glistening in the sun, fifty-foot swimming pool, red clay tennis court, twenty princely rooms and not one of them Cole's. I liked it better that way naturally. But she didn't. She threw it open to itinerant tennis players, fed us, harbored us, honored us, kept herself busy with us. She was unfailingly gracious. Never guilty of self-pity. Never accusatory. Grateful to Cole, she insisted, for delivering her from her nunnery. And yet, to me, she seemed like a woman derailed, as if the thrust of her life were meant for another set of tracks. So I wondered if she ever wondered how it might have been for her if Daddy had not gone wheeling and dealing to Tanganyika at the particular time he did.

"Hello, Matty dear," she said, leaning into the car window to kiss my cheek. Then, having given the orders that would dispose of my suitcases and tennis rackets, she turned back to me. "Do you want to get settled now, or have a drink with me first? There is something I'd like to talk to you about."

"In that case, drink with you first," I said, and followed her into the massive, oak-beamed room that functioned as a den. It was a room I'd always loved, comfortable and welcoming. Its sliding glass door led directly to Elinore's garden, and beyond this, by an earthen downhill path almost concealed by shrubbery, to the swimming pool about a hundred yards away. Standing at the door I could see just an edge of green water sparkling. I opened the door and breathed deeply.

"Garden smells nice," I said. "As ever." I crossed the room, took the martini she'd made for me, and kissed her again. "So do you smell nice. As ever. Thank you for inviting me."

"It's always good to have you here, Matty. You know that."

"Who else have you asked? I know about Berto."

"The usual—Timmy, Ann, and Wally. But this is only Friday, and since the tournament doesn't start until Wednesday there may be one or two others dropping in." She hesitated briefly. "There usually are," she added.

I knew who she was hoping for and kept my mouth shut.

"Ann's bringing Joe Farragut," she said. "Do you know him at all well?"

"He interviewed me once. It was a dopey interview. Is he what you wanted to talk about?"

"No. That is, I do, but there's something else first. Meg's here."

Once again I kept my mouth shut. That is, I think I did. But it might have dropped open a little.

"She's working for me. As my secretary."

"Do you need a secretary?"

"As a matter of fact I do. I really do. I'm a rich woman, and one of the things about money is it generates activity. A lot of people want it, you see. A good secretary simplifies life enormously. I know because the one before Meg was dreadful."

"In contrast to Meg?"

"Does that really surprise you?"

"Meg working for you surprises me. After that nothing surprises me."

"Because of what happened between Meg and Cole? Would you say that was Meg's fault?"

"Would you say it was rape?"

"You know, you're a very nice man, Matty. I mean your instincts are good, and there's no real malice or cruelty in you. And, of course, you're very attractive. All of which sometimes makes me forget how dense you can be."

I found myself smiling. "How am I being dense?"

"What seems obvious about what happened that night . . . three *years* ago . . . is that four people were to blame. And since you and I were two of them, it ill befits us to cast stones."

"Forgive and forget."

"Yes."

"Are you that Christian?"

"I am that civilized."

"I know you are," I said after a moment, and turned away from her to look out into the garden again. "I'm lousy at flowers. What's that big, red job, the one with the pointed leaves?"

She ignored this. "At any rate, Meg's been with me for almost three months, and I've become quite fond of her. Knowing you'd be here, she wanted to go away until the tournament was over, but I insisted that she not. You're both adults. There's no reason you can't be civil to each other. Besides it's a big house in which it's easily possible for you to keep out of each other's way if you've a mind to. Are you listening to me, Matty?"

"Yes."

"I just wanted to be sure."

"How did she come to you? I mean the last I heard she was working for some big New York ad agency."

"Something happened there."

"What? According to Berto, she was delighted with herself because she'd found something she could earn a living at. She was all full of Women's Lib and vinegar."

"Very funny."

"And she was going with some guy."

"Yes."

"He was married. What are you grinning at?"

"You have kept tabs, haven't you?"

I shrugged. "Berto runs off at the mouth sometimes. It's hard to stop him."

"Well, I don't know what happened at the agency. We haven't talked much about it. At any rate, we bumped into each other in town and decided to have lunch. She told me she was between jobs, and I got the sense of somebody very much wanting something to keep busy at, and so, on impulse, I told her I was between secretaries. Then one thing led to another. Now . . . aren't you going to ask me?"

"Ask you what?"

"How she feels about you these days?"

"I am not going to ask you that. What I'm going to ask you to do is change the subject."

"Ambivalent."

"That's fascinating."

"As ambivalent about you as I'd guess you are about her."

"Tell me about Farragut. Is Ann serious about him? Could she be?"

"Why?"

"Speaking of ambivalence, he's queer, isn't he?"

"Is he?"

"If you mean has he made a pass at me, the answer is no. But I've heard informed talk. Not a lot, but some. Is that what you're trying to find out?"

She looked a shade uncomfortable. "Yes, I suppose so. Ann worries me. But then Ann has always worried me. She has that beautiful, bland face. And that blandness is so marvelous for her because whatever it is you think she's thinking, you're always wrong."

"*You're* always wrong."

"Not you?"

"No, ma'am. Because, dense though I may be, I see her for the simple, uncomplicated, greedy child she really is. You tend to romanticize her. She has one guiding principle, your Annie, just one."

"That's such a terrible over-simplification."

"What's in it for me? Usually this translates into how *much* is in it for me? Your Annie loves money."

"Why shouldn't she? To her, it means survival."

"I'm not blaming her for anything. I'm merely trying to indicate that if you want to worry about someone, it probably should be Farragut. Unless, of course, he knows what he's doing, too. Because, surer than hell, Ann does."

She sighed. "Well, anyway, she's coming tomorrow. And she's asked that she and Mr. Farragut be supplied with adjoining rooms. And that you be assigned to the other side of her."

"Me? Why?"

"I don't know. Don't you know?"

I was silent for a moment, considering. "Maybe she wants to be protected from some former lover or other."

She glanced at me, a touch disdainfully. "Aren't you a former lover?"

"We parted friends. Very uncomplicated. Just a—"

"Spare me, please."

"Consider yourself spared."

She studied me for a moment, then came close enough to put her hand on my cheek. "I'm sorry. I didn't mean to be abrupt . . . with you of all people, Matty. You've always been so sweet to me."

"That's not hard."

"I'm glad you're the first to arrive," she said, smiling.

"Berto's driving up with Timmy after the South Orange tournament, but I guess you know that. Dot Magruder's there, too, only she's got her own car. Wally called to say he'd be here, but he didn't say when. So we'll probably have a nice quiet dinner tonight." She'd taken my hand to lead me toward the staircase, but now, at the foot of it, she stopped. The rush of words stopped, too. She looked at me imploringly. There was no way I could avoid being cruel. No way, short of lying, which I was tempted to do but decided against on the grounds that it would have been the ultimate cruelty.

"The last time I saw him was at Merion. No, he didn't say anything you'd want to hear."

"What *did* he say?"

"Nothing."

"Matty, please."

"For God's sake, you've got to get that bastard out of your mind. There's just no point in anything else."

Her eyes turned hot. "What do you know about it? You don't know anything about Cole at all."

"Don't I?"

"No. You see him one way, in one dimension, and that's it as far as you're concerned. That's enough for you. The fact that this distorts the view doesn't bother you at all. Nor does it keep you and everybody like you from explaining him to me. But I don't have to listen, you see. Wouldn't I be stupid if I did? I've known Cole Cooper since he was ten. I watched him grow up. I know things about Cole Cooper that nobody in this world can know. And some of them are good things, wonderful things. There are bad things in Cole? Is that supposed to be a revelation to me? Don't be a fool, Matty."

"All right."

"And don't protect me. I don't need protecting. I'm very strong, and I'm very patient. And I see something very clearly that you can't. I see that he'll come back to me some day."

"All right, Elinore."

"He will."

"Okay."

"No, I mean it, he will. Matty, ask yourself—could a man be as aggressive as Cole is unless he is also terribly vulnerable. Isn't that the other side of it? He attacks . . . he attacks constantly, but why? Because he's so appallingly open to attack himself. Because he's terrified that if he doesn't attack things . . . people . . . will hurt *him*. How could he feel otherwise? You don't know . . . and I can only guess . . . what those ten years with that dreadful father of his were really like. But I've heard his nightmares. I've held him in my arms to comfort and quiet him. A long time ago, yes, but you don't forget things like that. I mean he won't either. And one day he'll need me desperately enough to come back to me. I know he will."

I kept silent.

"He has to," she said, and ran ahead of me up the stairs.

The phone was ringing in my room when I got there, and, lifting it, I found myself listening to a voice I'd never heard before, explaining that he was a producer for the *Today Show* and was trying to put together a program in connection with the U. S. Open. Would I be available for an appearance?

"All right," I said, willingly enough. It's part of the job to promote tennis as much as possible, and most of us accept it as such. Self-defeating not to. Lines the pockets. "When?"

"Let's see, the tournament begins Wednesday, that's September 2, right? And it ends Sunday, September 13. Will you be in the finals?"

"Are you kidding?"

"Well, I know you can't be absolutely certain. But can't you project?"

"Project what? My chances through seven matches against the best players in the world? That's what I'd have to do."

"I see. And you can't?"

"No, I can't," I said, irritation mounting.

"Well, all right, suppose we schedule you and your colleagues for Friday, September 11. It'll be our last show before the finals. Actually, we're kind of building it around one of your superstars . . . a kind of informal *This is Your Life*, tennis-wise. I mean all his closest friends. People like you, Timmy Clark, Chris Hazlett . . ."

"Whose closest friends?"

"Didn't I mention that?"

"No."

"Why Cole Cooper's, of course."

After a moment: "What did you say your name was?"

"Didn't I mention that either?"

"No."

"Smithfield. Hamilton Smithfield."

"I see. And now, Mr. Smithfield, would you put Mr. Ramirez on the phone?"

Smothered laughter, followed by the clown himself. He said, "Ah, when Berto pulls ze leg, ze leg she is well pulled."

"Who was ze voice?"

"An amigo from the local radio station. How goes it with you *compadre?*"

"It goes. Haven't seen you in a while. When are you and Timmy coming up?"

"Monday, probably. Timmy finds himself a finalist."

"And you were not so lucky?"

"No, *compadre*. The game, she is not what she was. She creaks and groans and splits a little at the seams. That baby gringo from Texas, Dawson, he takes me out in the quarters, straight sets." It was said with obligatory lightness, in the Ramirez manner, but I sensed the unhappiness. It was my unhappiness, every aging pro's unhappiness, when a bad day, or infinitely worse, a bad season delivers intimations of mortality. Berto's season had been as abysmal as mine. And even more disappointing, I guess, since just the year before he'd been champion at Wimbledon and a semi-finalist at Forest Hills. My year before, though adequate, had been considerably less flamboyant.

"Say Rosewall and Gonzales fifty times tonight before you go to sleep."

"That will help my misbegotten backhand?"

"No," I sighed, "but maybe it'll help you sleep."

Suddenly he laughed. "Matty, it is Cole against Timmy in the finals here, did you know that?"

"Certainly not. After Merion I declared myself a two-week moratorium on tennis. No playing, no even reading about it. I'm desperate."

"But, Matty, it is like a war. There has been a disintegration."

"There could not have been a disintegration."

"Yes, believe me, there has been. Whereas it was once only hate between those two, now there is blood lust. If someone were to take their rackets from them and substitute *pistolas*, they would use them joyfully."

"Sounds ugly."

"Ugly—and yet, forgive me, funny, too. In the sense that fanatics are merely zanies turned inside out. Or is that just me, *compadre*?"

"Well, I see what you mean, but I don't have your detachment. My sympathies are all with Timmy. I hope he slaughters the enemy."

"Sympathies? Ah, that is something else again. May the arm of Timmy Clark be strong and true so that he can smite the white devil a smite heard round the world."

"Beautiful."

"Puerto Rican and black solidarity forever. Revenge against the Wasp. Not you, though. You are a Wasp of color."

"Thanks. Berto . . ."

"*Sí, compadre?*"

"Meg's here."

A moment of silence. "I know," he said. "She wrote that she would be. How does it sit with you?"

"It sits heavily. And I haven't even seen her yet."

"It sits heavily with her, too. So she said. But perhaps that's a good sign."

"Of what?"

"My sainted grandmother had a phrase for it. The woman who sits heavily bears fat, healthy *muchachos*."

"I'll give that the serious attention it no doubt deserves."

"You could do worse. You could do far worse. Until to-morrow, *compadre*."

"*Adiós*."

I set about unpacking my things and thinking about Berto —and Meg—as I did. Thinking about Meg was pointless, since it led to a familiar blank wall against which my head had banged frequently enough to cause specific tenderness. I decided to do myself a favor and *stop* thinking about Meg. This was made a little easier than it might have been by the fact that I was somewhat disturbed about Berto. He hadn't seemed right. He had seemed . . . what, worried? Maybe. Maybe less than that. But not right. Berto was my cherished friend, and I was sensitive to him the way a man often was who, out of general dourness, did not make friends easily. Berto did, but I didn't. Berto was the much loved, exceedingly pampered oldest son of a prominent Puerto Rican family. His mother told me once that in her opinion he was the most spoiled child in San Juan. And then she added, "But how could he not be? He is so beautiful." Many women had found him so. His face was patrician thin, high cheekboned, imperiously nosed. He had thick black hair, eyes the color of patent leather buttons, a cleft in his chin, and skin like copper. He was only five feet six, but classically proportioned. Very strong, and, on the tennis court, explosive—a watch-charm warrior who fought for each point as if the lives of his loved ones depended on it; scrambling, tumbling, giving up on nothing. In his seventeen years of big-time tennis—here and abroad—he'd been the gallery's darling wherever he'd appeared. And he exulted in this. Berto was a born actor, with an actor's frenzy for applause. It energized him, sustained him, and when, after one of his typically outlandish retrieves, it rolled toward him adoringly, he seemed to swell with it, become majestic. And then his opponent, not Berto, had to be giant-killer to win.

He was sharp-witted, sharp-tongued, and nerveless. He was afraid of nothing and no one. We had become friends, in fact, on the day I helped rescue him from a pair of anti-student Angelenos, neither of whom outweighed him by less than thirty pounds. It was in a bar, far enough from the campus to qualify as no-man's land. They had called him dago, and, choosing to disregard the inaccuracy, he had attacked. With two acquaintances I was in the adjoining room. I'd been made aware of what was happening when Berto was hit hard enough to be knocked from one room to the other and land, spread-eagled, across my table. *"Gracias, señor,"* he'd said as I'd helped him to his feet. Then, grinning through a spatter of blood, he'd staggered back toward the eager Angelenos. There was, in Berto, that quality that aroused immediate partisanship. Hesitating only long enough to grab a beer bottle, I'd followed him. So had my acquaintances. Four to two, instead of two to one. The fun went out of it for the Angelenos. They'd fled—Berto screaming after them, "I am a spic not a dago, you Angeleno dung."

We were a study in contrasts, Berto and I. He was open, I was shut—though not so firmly as I'd once been, thank God. His background was affluence, mine penny-nursing. His parents had worshiped him, mine had suffered me. I was the third boy in a family of five who'd hit on tennis luckily and got lucky, in turn, because of it. On the surface I had much more in common with Cole Cooper, and yet, from the day we'd met, there'd been this kindredness between Berto and me. I was thankful for it. I recognized its worth to me. We'd become doubles partners and eventually roommates. Through the years, between us, we'd won a lot of tennis matches for U.C.L.A. and then for America's Davis Cup team. We'd chased a lot of chicks, drunk a lot of booze, and, on and off the courts, shared a lot of intense moments, the memory of which would be better than a fireplace to keep my old bones warm.

I did not see Berto these days as much as I once had. Of necessity, new patterns had formed for both of us when I married Meg, and they'd grown strong enough to maintain themselves, as patterns will, after the rupture. Berto was a lodestone for people. Given a vacuum, new friends had moved into it, among them, recently, Meg herself, who saw him now as much as I did. So the exclusivity of our friendship was past. But the kindredness remained, and thus he could not hide it from me—nor I from him, for that matter —when something troubled. He was superb, however, at hiding precisely what that might be. I have said he was open. Generally, he was—and yet when it came to a certain category of vital interests he could wrap himself in a cloak of Spanish impenetrability. And he held the key to this category. That is, he defined it. To me, it was always enigma. Nevertheless, I examined a grab bag of possibilities. By the time I discarded them all as idle speculation, I had finished unpacking. Then I began thinking of Meg again. Would she be joining us for dinner, I wondered. And, predictably, I could not decide if I wanted her to or not.

Not is what it turned out to be. Elinore volunteered no explanation, and I asked for none. She seemed abstracted, gracious as always, but far away. The quiet dinner she'd promised was quiet indeed. And brief. She barely made it through coffee and then asked to be excused.

"Migraine," she said. "Go walk in the garden, Matty. Or

take a swim. Please do something pleasant, so that I can forgive myself for being such rotten company."

"Can I help?"

"With what?"

"I mean is anything wrong?"

"Wrong? No." For a moment, it seemed as if she would add to this, but she changed her mind. She turned and left.

So I went walking in the garden and found Meg picnicking there. She sat on a bench, sandwich in her lap, papers that looked like correspondence spread out next to her. She wore a man's shirt with rolled-up sleeves and jeans. No make-up. Eyeglasses shoved up on top of her hair. She shattered me. She obliterated my quandary. I knew, instantly, that I was as safe from her as your average snake is from your average mongoose. When I was reasonably sure my voice would be steady, I said, "You have egg salad on your upper lip."

She licked it away. "How are you, Matty?"

"Why didn't you have dinner with us? Didn't Elinore explain how two grown people can be depended on to be civil to each other?"

"I had work to do," she said, indicating the papers.

"Did you think I'd make a scene?"

"No, really, Matty, I have all these letters to be answered. If they're not answered right away, they pile up and—" She broke off.

"Okay," I said.

"You look well," she said.

"Thanks."

"I wasn't trying to avoid you."

"Okay."

"All right, I was."

"Why?"

Rival expressions battled in her face. One was laughter, and it won. "What's so funny?" I said.

"We are. We're ridiculous. Just listen to us. We haven't seen each other in almost three years, and it's as if we've never been apart. We're absurd. But then we always were, weren't we?"

"No," I said, and walked away from her, down the path that led to the swimming pool. I stayed there fifteen minutes or so, staring at the water, splitting the time between despising myself and her. When I came back up the path, she was gone. "Good riddance," I said like I meant it.

Saturday morning, early, feeling the need, I ended my tennis moratorium. I went down to the equipment shack to get myself a bucket of balls. We called it the equipment shack, but this was a playful misnomer. Actually, it was a roomy wooden structure which Elinore had thoughtfully furnished to serve us as a lounge as well—a fully stocked mahogany bar, throw rugs, a sofa, two leather easy chairs, plus extra rackets and a ton of practice balls. I loaded the bucket and took it with me to the court.

Serving drill was what I had in mind. God knew I could use some. My erstwhile cannon first service had petered to a popgun, and even at that I wasn't getting it in too often. You can't move to the net behind a popgun. And if you can't move to the net at Forest Hills, that's an epitaph in itself.

It would be August-hot later, but now it was only warm, comfortable. The red clay of the court looked invitingly springy. Therapeutic for an old bloke like me. I began hitting tennis balls, experimenting over and over again with the height of the toss, seeking there for my lost fire power. After a while I was drenched in sweat. That felt good. After a longer while my body found a rhythm. That felt even better. Balls tracered over the net to land deep in the box. "Yeah, you bastard," I said aloud to my prodigal cannon, "but where will you be when I need you?"

"Are you talking to me?"

I turned to see Meg sitting crosslegged in the grass behind

the fence. I felt so good I grinned at her. She grinned also, but then banished it as too risky. I understood that. I hit one more experimental twist, saw it kick high and in to my right-handed foe, and went over to sit next to her.

"You foot-faulted," she said.

"The umpire didn't see it. It's that old lady who used to fall asleep at Wimbledon. What was her name?"

"I forget."

"How are you this morning?"

She shut her eyes and lifted her face in obeisance to the sun. "Ah," she said, making it a long, grateful sound. She wore shorts and a halter and sneakers over bare feet so I said, "Do you ever play this game any more?"

"With Elinore occasionally, when I can drag her out. She doesn't really like it, you know."

"Is your racket in the shack?"

"Yes."

"Well?"

She hesitated a moment, then nodded and went to get it. We whacked balls back and forth for almost an hour, just rallying, nothing serious. Meg always could keep the ball in play. Fine ground strokes, and she could cover the court. It was her spottiness at the net that had caused her problems against the likes of Dot Magruder.

So we ran and gamboled in the sun and were very nice to each other. "Great shot" and "beautiful get" we kept saying to each other. Safe, functional conversation that would have seen us through, all right, if the tennis goddess had behaved decently. She didn't. She infrequently does. She caused me to be at the net when Meg scorched a shot that clipped the tape and then the corner of my eye. It stung. But I dropped my racket not so much in pain as in panic. Flashing before me was this apocalyptic image of myself permanently blinded. Like Wally. My career in shreds. My backhand relegated to a tin cup. As the racket dropped, Meg screamed and came running.

"Oh, God," she said, pushing my hand away from the eye so that she could look. "Matty, are you all right? Please say you're all right."

"How the hell can I?"

"I mean can you see out of it at all?"

"No."

"*Open* it."

"No."

"*Please.* We won't be able to tell anything unless you do."

Unwillingly, I obeyed. And then instantly I knew it was nothing serious. Blurred vision, yes, but already this was clearing. And the pain was diminishing. From all affected sectors, my body was telegraphing reassurances, which, for reasons of my own, I chose not to receive immediately. But I couldn't fool Meg.

"Grace under pressure," she said, laughing in relief. "You're such a baby."

"Thanks."

"Well, you are. Carrying on that way and scaring me half to death."

Now that my eye was definitely out of danger, it was my feelings that were hurt. "With a little effort, you might manage to understand," I muttered.

"I understand, all right. I've *always* understood. Tennis—the be-all and the end-all. And anything that threatens your tennis threatens your life because nothing else matters a damn to you. Who should understand that better than I?"

"For Christ's sake, it's my business."

"Liar," she said. She spoke the word with immense bitterness, and started walking off the court. Then, suddenly, she stopped and turned back to me. "It's your religion. Or it's your wife and mistress all rolled into one. But it's nothing as uncomplicated as your business. Don't lie to me. I can't stand it when you lie to me." She turned again. This time she was running. I called to her. Halfheartedly, because I knew she wouldn't stop.

When I got back to the house after returning the bucket to the equipment shack, I found company. Ann Cronin and Joe Farragut had arrived. They were in the den, tall glasses already in hand. Elinore, abstinent, was with them. When Ann saw me she squealed with more or less honest delight and hurried forward to kiss and hug. Hugging Ann was always a back-to-nature experience. It was like hugging Mother Earth. She was a big, bountiful brunette, built like an adolescent's fantasy. Brassieres were anathema to her, so that when she walked she jiggled, prow and stern. Not that there was anything sloppy about Ann. She was just a lot of woman, all of it delicious. She glowed with health. Her skin was creamy. Framed by short, naturally curly hair, her face was as guileless as a 4-H Club winner's. Round, pink-cheeked, snub-nosed, eyes like blue crayons. And none of this meant a thing, of course. Not if you knew her.

"Lover," she said. "Oh, lover, it's been so long." Her accent was like Cole's, off again, on again at will. "I've been starved for the very sight of you, I do declare."

"It's been two weeks," I said, smiling. Somehow you almost always smiled when Ann was around. It was a reflex. But at the same time, if you had any sense, you kept painfully alert. That was a conditioned reflex.

"An age, an absolute age," she said, and kissed me again. Then, tucking my arm snugly into her side, she led me into the room proper. "Isn't two weeks an age, Joe, when it's that long since you've seen your heart's delight?"

"An eon," he said obediently.

"You know Joe Farragut, don't you, Matty?"

"Yes," I said.

"Of course," he said. "Did a piece on him once. First-rate piece it was, wasn't it, Matty?"

Sure it was, I thought, if you admired turgid prose from a writer whose sense of tennis was haphazard at best—so much so that after reading his piece I'd wondered if he'd ever swung a racket in anger. Certainly, he didn't know the difference between top and underspin. Still, he'd meant to be kind, and I decided not to play critic. That was the thing about Farragut. Though, like Wally, he was a rich man's son, though he had the dilettante's capacity to irritate the professional, you usually ended by feeling sorry for him. He was a tall man in his early forties. Not blatantly homosexual, just a shade willowy. It was in his walk and, on occasion, in the way he moved his hands. He had sparse blond hair, a wispy beard, and brown eyes that were gentle and anxious by turns. Right now they beamed good will at me through the thick lenses of his rimless glasses. As I shook his hand, I wondered what Ann had in mind for him.

"Would you like something to drink?" Elinore asked. "There's some orange juice in that pitcher on the table."

"Some gin, too," Ann said.

"Shame on you," I said. "This hour of the morning."

"I'm in training starting Monday, not before. The weekend's mine, lover."

"To dissipation," Farragut said, raising his glass and beaming his glance around the room—a silent appeal for us to laugh.

"Mmmm," Ann said, as she kissed me one final time before releasing me. "Y'all smell so nice and sweaty . . . a little like one of Elinore's studs. Remember them, Elinore, and how marvelously erotic it used to feel whenever we sneaked down to the stable?"

"I never sneaked down to the stable. And I wasn't aware you did either."

"Weren't you?" Now she went to Elinore to deliver another quota of hugs and kisses. "Oh, well, there was lots you weren't aware of. Because we didn't want to hurt you, you see. All of us being so bad, and you being so good, little Mommy."

Elinore pushed her away—and yet she, too, was smiling. "Ann, you're impossible. Restrain yourself. You're deliberately putting on a show."

"Am I?"

"Yes."

"Well, I *can't* restrain myself. It's much too beautiful a day for that kind of ickiness. Restraint! Pooh!" Then, turning back to me and grinning wickedly, she said, "Elinore tells me Meg's here. Let's scandalize her good."

"Now that's enough," Elinore said, truly outraged. "Ann, go on up to your room and take a pill of some kind. You're behaving appallingly."

"Like a bitch. I *am* part bitch, you know that. And besides, she deserves a pang or two from the green-eyed monster, that Meg. Doesn't she, Matty? Imagine her letting a beautiful thing like you get away from her. Joe wouldn't."

That was too much for Elinore. She rose and walked stiff-backed from the room, Ann in laughing pursuit. "Elinore, come back. I'm sorry. I won't be bad any more, I promise." She chased Elinore up the stairs, and we heard her voice, cajoling and apologizing, until a door closed it off. An uncomfortable silence. I looked at Farragut and saw the hot color in his cheeks.

"Not very delicate, is she?" he said.

"No. That's not what she's famous for."

"I try not to let it bother me, but it does, you know. She does that kind of thing often. Why are some people so heedless of other people's feelings?"

"I can't answer that."

"You've known her a long time, haven't you?"

"Seven, eight years or so."

He nodded. "Ever since she came up from Virginia with Cole, Wally, and Timmy."

"Yes."

He was silent a moment. "It's fascinating, isn't it, how much they're alike."

"Who?"

He seemed surprised that I hadn't followed. "Why Cole and Ann, of course. Neither of them gives a damn about anyone else's feelings. And then they're both so attractive, aren't they?"

"I think I'll head for the shower," I said. "Have they shown you your room yet?"

"Yes. I'm all unpacked."

"Then I'll see you later."

"Matty . . ."

"Yes?"

"Did Ann tell you we were engaged?"

"No," I said. "She did not."

He smiled. "I know what you're thinking. You're thinking what a curious pairing, a girl like Ann and me. But you see I'm perfectly normal, really. That was merely Ann's way of teasing me."

"All right," I said.

"I just wanted you to know. Because you've always been very decent to me. Others haven't, but you have. You've not leaped to conclusions. You've kept an open mind. Others . . . well, I know I have some . . . mannerisms that suggest effeminacy, but I assure you that's an accident of my physical structure. I assure you I am quite, *quite* normal. At least as normal as . . ." He broke off and suddenly his expression changed. All the upward lines swooped downward. "This is a very strange conversation, isn't it?" he said unhappily.

I kept silent, watching him.

He sighed. "It's not eleven o'clock yet, and I've had three gins."

"That will do it."

"If I'm not careful I'll have a drinking problem by the time I'm forty-five."

"So be careful."

"That's all I need," he said, "a drinking problem."

"*Are* you and Ann engaged?"

"No." He turned away to cross the room to the glass door. "I also have a lying problem."

I left him staring gloomily out at the garden, as if he saw there a cemetery for dead illusions.

Sunday morning I managed to coax Ann onto the court for some brisk hitting, after which I declined her invitation to visit South Orange for Cooper versus Clark. She was going with Farragut, and Ann versus Farragut was an exhibition I thought I could do without. As I watched them drive off together it occurred to me that Joe Farragut was one of those people who aroused sympathy in absentia. The idea of him was sad enough, but seeing him leave was one of life's minor pleasures. I had the house to myself. Meg and Elinore were off garden-partying in support of a local political candidate. Elinore had seemed excited. No hint of Cooper-induced migraine. Good, I told myself hopefully. Maybe he's losing his clout. Dreamer, I told myself, pragmatism reasserting its hold in the next moment. In the shower, I toyed with the notion of a solo visit to South Orange. Once more I decided against the trip. I felt pleasantly lazy. In the end, I did some reading, wrote some letters, listened to some music, sunned by poolside, filled the day with gentle strokes and was reasonably content.

On Monday I moved my practice program to the grass at Forest Hills and was pleased at continued signs of progress. The serve, in particular. I was beginning to get the feeling I might be able to trust it again. A terrific feeling. Like being reunited with a comrade in arms. So up was I, that even the prospect of meeting with Wally seemed less dismal than it usually did. We were supposed to meet in his office, but he had called and switched to a bar he liked on Fifty-seventh Street. A year after he'd stopped playing competitively, Wally had turned to agentry. Not for the money, certainly, but to have something to do that was close to tennis. When he'd asked to represent me, I hadn't been able to say no. Cole had been able to—some cock and bull story about a commitment he couldn't get out of. The truth was Cole knew—as I did—that Wally would be lousy at it. And Cole's streak of sentiment was wide enough to slide neatly through a needle's eye. So Wally had this plush Fifth Avenue office, which he avoided as much as possible because it reminded him of what a terrible businessman he was. And three clients. Berto, me, and, oddly enough, Ann. Ann's sentimental streak was about as thick as Cole's, I would have sworn, and yet there she was.

Wally ordered me a gin and tonic and told me about the testimonial he'd set up for me with a sporting goods manufacturer . . . specifically an aluminum racket. I told him I'd heard the company was on the brink of bankruptcy. That was news to him, he said. It wasn't news to very many others, I said patiently, and consequently I wasn't sure I wanted my name associated. Would he check it out? He said he would, and all the time we talked he kept looking at his watch. That puzzled me. We were due at an ad agency for preliminary discussions on another testimonial possibility . . . the purpose of my trip into town . . . but that was an hour away. I pointed this out to him.

"Matty, would you mind taking that on alone?" he said. "It's just preliminary. You could find out what they're offering, and we could discuss it later. You wouldn't mind, would you?"

"Why? Has something come up?"

"Well, the fact is, yes." He hesitated. Then, not looking at me, he said, "The fact is Cole called as soon as I hung up after talking to you this morning. He's having motor trouble, and he has to leave his car in the repair shop, so he asked me to drive down to South Orange to pick him up."

"When?"

"In a little while."

"No one else in the whole world has transportation?"

"Well, he asked *me*."

I kept silent, and he knew I wasn't pleased. "I don't blame you for being sore," he said. "I wanted to say no, I really did. I started to say no, but before I knew it it came out yes. It always does." He looked so unhappy that I couldn't stay angry with him.

"Don't sweat it," I said. "I'll make out. And you're right, plenty of time to discuss details later."

"Hell of an agent I am," he said gloomily.

"We're doing all right."

"Matty, *why* can't I say no to him? I mean he treats me like dirt, and I make all these rules about what I won't do any more. And then I just go ahead and do what I always do. Why is that?"

It was a question worth speculating about, but what I chose to say was, "I don't know."

"I do," he said. "Because I'm a jerk." And then, suddenly, he slammed his glass down on the bar hard enough to shatter it. It didn't shatter, but it should have. The bartender shot him a glance of professional disdain. The dozen or so other patrons in the room terminated desultory conversations and focused on him hopefully. He ignored them all. "*Christ*," he said as if he were alone, "he's so goddam rotten to me."

"Calm down," I said. "You're attracting attention."

He looked around in surprise. Then, taking a deep breath, he said, "I'm sorry."

"Nothing to be sorry about. Just take it easy."

"Matty . . ."

"What?"

"I think there's going to be some trouble."

"What kind of trouble?"

"I'm driving him to Elinore's."

"She'll be glad to see him," I said grimly.

"He sounded as if he had something in mind. Something . . . I don't know . . . unpleasant."

I kept silent.

"What are you thinking?"

"Me? I'm thinking that if I were smart, I'd double back to that house right now, grab my bags, and go somewhere else."

"And yet sometimes he can be so nice."

"So I've been told."

"You wouldn't believe how nice he can be when he tries, when he really wants to be."

"No, I wouldn't," I said. "And I'll go on not believing it, no matter how many times I hear otherwise."

"Ah, Matty."

"Finish your drink."

A few minutes later he left, and I had one more to fortify myself against the hot three-block walk to the ad agency.

When I got back to the house around five-thirty Cole was there. I heard his laugh, mean and mocking, as I put my hand to the door of the den. Reflexively, I withdrew it. I almost withdrew myself as well, but I was sticky and thirsty again, and had been thinking gin and tonic for the past half hour. "Drop dead, Cooper," I said to myself as a rallying cry, and twisted the knob.

As if the pace of events had given a sudden lurch forward, the cast was all but assembled. Only Timmy and Ann were absent. Ann was probably sleeping one off, and Timmy was probably elsewhere in the house, in self-exile, since where Cole was Timmy tried hard not to be. A good rule. In addition to Elinore, Meg, and Farragut, there were Berto, Dot Magruder, and Wally. In center court—the star engirt by these minor luminaries—Cole. At least that's the way it looked at first glance, a set piece out of feudalism; the petty chiefs gathered to pay fealty to—and receive the law from—old King Cole himself. Or it was a party; a curiously joyless party, in which tight-lipped guests stared stonily into their drinks with only one voice raised in laughter. If it could be called laughter, if anything could be called laughter that was so manifestly intended to hurt.

"Now you listen to me, Magruder," he was saying in Dixie-plus as I unobtrusively closed the door behind me and leaned against it. "Now you listen hard, hear? You want to beat Annie? You want to win yourself that coveted grand slam? Lay off sex. I mean *entirely*. I mean, during the *entire* tournament. Now we all know how hard that's going to be for you. But sex drains you, Magruder. It does for a fact. So you be good, little girl. And that'll give you a clear-cut edge. It surely will, I do declare. Because Annie here . . . there ain't no way she won't grind herself to a frazzle."

Like a hammer, his laughter rose again to smash at our ears. I saw Meg wince and Elinore bite her lip. Berto looked straight ahead. Farragut looked sad. Wally smiled . . . he forced himself to smile. The laugh rang out against our silence; a silence ugly and uncomfortable, the silence of accessories. But we hoped it wasn't a major crime, you see. We hoped Dot wasn't minding too much.

"Well, now, here's Matty just in time," Cole said, choosing to become aware of my existence. "You'll help, won't you, old buddy? I mean you'll do your best to maintain self-discipline. The Lord knows she's tempting . . . a mantrap, by God. But it's for her own good, right?"

Dot was anything but a mantrap, of course. She was not really homely either—all the features cleanly shaped and pleasantly in proportion. But it's true it took a while to notice this because her physique compelled such avid attention. She was a large, rectangle of a woman. An inch under six feet, coming down in straight lines from a pair of barn-door shoul-

45

ders. She was like a plank, all her surfaces flat. In tennis costume, she looked ludicrous, deceptively benign, the way a dancing bear might. Early in her career, this had lulled more than one opponent into euphoria, only to find herself a set down and shockingly aware of how punishing a player Magruder really was. Dot affected brittleness, talked tough, swore, told dirty jokes, in a desperate attempt to erect defenses. Actually, she was a nice enough not terribly bright girl, and we all knew this. Attacking her had become a taboo among us. She had grown used to being protected, so that what was happening to her now left her pitifully unprepared to cope.

But finally I pushed myself away from the wall and moved into the room. I moved very close to Cole. "Stop it," I said.

"But it's a joke, Matty, old buddy. Just a joke, that's all. Now don't tell me you all thought I was serious? Dot, did you think I was serious?"

She kept silent. She had to. She was too close to tears to risk speech. "Well, I'll be a suckhead mule," Cole said, projecting wonderment. "In this group, of all groups, I would have sworn to Jesus a man could do a joke and get a groovy response from an *appreciative* audience." He grinned and let his gaze move slowly and purposefully from me to Berto and back again. And then, of course, I understood. It was his revenge for the threatening letters, exacted through Dot because he knew it would be more painful that way. I glanced at Berto and saw that he understood, too. And maybe had from the beginning. He looked pale and murderous.

As if emerging from a broken trance, Elinore shook her head back and forth sharply and then moved from her chair to the sofa, next to Dot. She took Dot's hand but spoke to Cole. "If it was a joke, it was a dreadful joke," she said. "A little like pulling wings off flies. Which is something I don't recall you doing when you were small."

To my surprise, it smarted. I saw Cole's eyes flicker for a

moment, but he recovered swiftly. "When they do unto you, little Mommy, you do unto them—harder. Sure enough."

"Right on," Dot said suddenly, surging to her feet like a submarine. Once there, she teetered back and forth for a moment, as if standing erect were something she would have to get used to again. Her eyes swept us frantically, her smile fixed and desperate. "Goddam right it was a joke. Hell with anybody who can't take a joke," she added, and ran blindly from the room.

Not for the first time, I wanted to hit Cole.

Silently, Elinore begged me not to.

"I better go to her," Meg said to Elinore, who nodded and turned to Cole again.

"There's not the slightest possibility you're enjoying this," she said.

"Isn't there?"

"You can fool these others, and perhaps even yourself, but not me. I know you too well. I see the self-hatred in it. For God's sake, Cole, why won't you let anyone help you?"

"Crud," he said. "Crud on crud on crud. That's why I left you, Elinore, because you talk such a lot of crud." But it surprised me again to see how angry he was.

Then Farragut sighed and got to his feet to leave, which was a mistake because it drew Cole's attention to him. "Hey, Farragut, want to be my ball boy?"

Farragut kept moving.

Cole cupped his hands around his mouth and shouted after him. "Some other time? When you're less *fagged?*"

"Cole, Cole," Elinore said, hopelessly.

He didn't look at her. His face was absolutely savage. "I'm going down to work on the backboard," he said. "It's the only goddam thing around here that's not full of crud." ·

"I'll change my clothes and get my racket," Wally said. "What for?"

Wally knew something bad was about to happen to him;

you could tell from the way he scrunched up, as a man will, sometimes, when a punch is telegraphed. But he said, "I'll hit some to you. It'll be better than the backboard."

"I *said* the backboard. Who needs you, cripple?"

There is no preparation for a thing like that, and as Cole went out—the exit of a poltergeist—Wally sagged visibly. Like a bruised child's, his glance sought Elinore's. Her glance was unavailable. Her eyes were shut, her head lowered, as if time had been called, and she must have the rest before she could cope again.

"Who cost me my eye?" Wally asked of no one in particular. And no one answered him.

Seconds trudged by. Then Berto said, "It was inspired, was it not, that whole performance?"

"Inspired?"

"In a way. He has a very fertile brain, that one."

"Where are you going?"

"To see if I can help Meg with Dot." But at the door he stopped. "*Compadre* . . . ?"

"Yes."

"Could you kill a man like that?"

"I might."

Two hours later, someone did.

CHAPTER 3

ENTER HOROWITZ

Meg and I found him. She had been knocking on doors, sent by Elinore, to see if anyone had seen him. No one had, not since he'd left the den. "Elinore's worried," she told me after she'd knocked on mine. "His clothes and things are still in his room, but he's not, and he's not down at the court." "Damn Elinore," I'd said but couldn't make it stick. So we'd formed our search party.

He was in the equipment shack. He was face down on the floor, naked, arms and legs flung wide. Something heavy had bashed in the base of his skull. There was blood all over his back and shoulders and on the floor, seeping into one of the throw rugs. I shut the door quickly, but Meg, a step behind me, had caught her glimpse.

"My God," she said. "Oh, my God."

"Are you all right?" I asked shakily.

She used a moment and then nodded.

"Stay here," I said.

"Why? I mean what are you going to do?"

I took a deep breath. "I have to make sure he's dead."

He was, of course. Dead and already turning cold. I straightened up from his body and went outside again. Meg, ashen, had propped herself against the side of the shack. "It's my knees," she said apologetically.

"One of us has to tell Elinore, one of us should call the police," I said.

"You tell Elinore. *Please?*"

"All right."

"I know that sounds cowardly, but you really are closer to her, aren't you?"

"Yes."

"Matty . . ."

"What?"

"He was naked, wasn't he?"

"Yes."

"Where were his clothes?"

"I don't know."

"Oh my God, what a stupid thing to say."

I took her hand. "Come, let's go."

We started back toward the house, slowly, reluctant to get there, neither of us speaking. When we reached it she stopped and turned to me. "Is this happening?" she asked.

She meant the question to be taken literally, as if the need was to gather evidence. I knew exactly what she was experiencing. "I touched his body," I said, addressing her but intending it for both of us.

As I climbed the stairs to Elinore's bedroom, I glanced at my watch—out of some subconscious urge, I suppose, to fix the time in order to buffer reality. It was ten minutes past ten. It was Monday, August 31. It was the last day of Cole Cooper's life. I announced all this to myself in an attempt to make myself feel something. I got no further than disbelief.

Two days later I believed it, all right. By that time I had seen enough of Lieutenant Jacob Horowitz, Nassau County Detective Bureau, to be *anchored* in reality. He was that kind of presence, as palpable as an elephant. Which, physically, was not an inept simile for him either. He was a huge man, six feet five, and ugly in a way . . . with such force . . . that somehow you found yourself quickly accepting this and then as quickly forgetting it. He shambled a little when he walked.

You got the feeling it was a manner of being careful. As if he had always been bigger and clumsier than everybody and had had to master techniques for avoiding unnecessary destruction. This did not mean, however, that you got the feeling he was gentle. Just careful. He had an easy, smiling, almost indolent way of asking questions, but his eyes worked ceaselessly. There was nothing gentle about his eyes. While his lips curved in smiles, his eyes watched voraciously, as if in a state of near starvation for the lies you would eventually set before them. He was in his early forties. Dark thinning hair, thick wings for eyebrows, sallow, slightly pock-marked complexion, and, like me, he had a scar. But his was much longer and more jagged than mine—the result, I learned later, of a knife wound while making an arrest. In all, when you looked at Jacob Horowitz, you saw a man you could readily construe as dangerous. When you knew him better you saw that he was aware of this, regarded it as a problem, and had developed an array of dissimulating tricks to lull you into underestimating him. He made me very nervous. So that when I came out of the locker room of the West Side Tennis Club that Wednesday morning I was less than delighted to see him waiting for me.

"You going to the funeral?" he asked.

"Yes."

"Come on, I'll give you a lift."

"No thanks. I came down with Berto. He'll drive me."

He gave me one of his indolent smiles. "This might save you a trip to headquarters."

"Was I planning a trip to headquarters?"

"Sooner or later."

I hesitated briefly. "I'll tell Berto," I said.

"Already told him."

We started off together, or rather not precisely together since, vaguely resentful, I refused to match his pace. He was a step and a half ahead of me when he stopped abruptly.

Tourist-like, he glanced around him. "First time I ever been here," he said. "Not bad."

And though he'd acknowledged this with modified enthusiasm, I suddenly found myself looking at it all through his eyes, that is a stranger's eyes. The West Side Tennis Club in Forest Hills—where I'd spent so much of the significant part of my life during the past seventeen years, where I'd been champion, where I'd been victimized. The West Side Tennis Club was a very complex, love-hate thing to me, so it was an eerie dislodgement to see it, for just those few moments, as land and structure, stripped of its emotional baggage. Not bad, he'd said. Hell, under the brilliant blue sky of this classic September day, it was magnificent. Blue sky, white-clad players, the grass richly green—not patchy the way it sometimes was—Forest Hills looked almost poignantly beautiful. And it looked thoroughly prepared for its great annual event to begin tomorrow when upward of ten thousand buffs would enliven its stands . . . a crowd that would swell to nearly fifteen thousand for the weekend play.

"You been here lots, I suppose," he said.

"Lots."

He turned toward me. "How come they didn't postpone the tournament?"

"Because of Cole?"

He nodded.

"They decided one day was enough." I paused, and then, as blandly as I could, said, "The tournament chairman decided Cole wouldn't have wanted more than that. It was in the newspapers. Don't you read the newspapers?"

"Yeah," he said, but didn't elaborate. Instead he said, "What do you do about the lost day?"

"Bunch up the matches a little, so that we can play the finals a week from Sunday as planned."

"You figure you got a chance to win?"

"If we're going, let's go," I said, and stepped out ahead of him.

"Listen," he said when he had caught up, "we both know I'm a *shmo* about tennis, so if I fall on my prat a time or two you have to bear with me. Now that makes sense, don't it?"

"All right."

"All *right*, so tell me this. How many matches do you play?"

"Seven, if I reach the finals."

"I see." And then he grinned at me. "And maybe as few as one," he said.

What that conjured up was the vision of a tall, talented young Frenchman with a daunting serve and an astonishing upset over Berto at Wimbledon. His name was Jean Boucher, and, as my first opponent, he would not be the soft touch you hoped for when your game was less than secure. The thought of him tightened my stomach and must have had a corresponding effect on my expression because, clearly, Horowitz enjoyed what he saw.

"You're a love, Horowitz," I said bitterly, and once more strode ahead of him.

The funeral home was in Manhasset, not far from Elinore's house, and, as we headed east into the city traffic—about which hostility was the only thing ever predictable—he said, "All of you going to the funeral?"

"All of who?"

"The guest list. The people staying at the house."

"I don't know." That wasn't so. I knew for a fact that Timmy wasn't because he'd told me so, but I was reluctant to acknowledge this.

"Mr. Clark isn't going," he said.

"Isn't he?"

He glanced at me, smiling. "The truth saves time, my wise

old grandfather used to say. Most of my people find that out sooner or later."

"Your people?"

"The people I deal with when I work on a case. I take a proprietary interest in them." Despite the traffic, he'd managed to catch the shift of expression in my face. It made him smile again. "I know even bigger words than that," he said. "What do you think cops are, dumb *shmos*? Would you like to risk a little something that as a group cops are smarter than tennis players?"

"You're not fond of tennis players?"

"Me? I'm fond of everybody. Tennis players aren't smart, but they're pretty. They should live and be well."

"Thanks."

We drove in silence for a moment. Then he said, "Cops don't kill each other. Right there, that makes them smarter than tennis players."

"You're sure one of us did?"

"Who else? The butler?" He chuckled in self-appreciation, and then he said, "Oh, we'll check out all possibilities, but I been working homicide going on twenty years, and I never seen such a collection of first-rate motives gathered under one roof. I mean really prime. Not one of you can be ruled out. Take you, for instance. You're going to the funeral because you're a mourner?"

"No."

"Big news. You're going for Mrs. Cooper's sake. Actually, he was kind of a jerk, wasn't he? Don't even bother to answer that. It's on record six ways to Sunday. And I'll tell you something else. If the motives are prime, the alibis are so lousy, I still can't get used to how lousy they are. I mean they don't exist. The Medical Examiner places his death between eight and eight-thirty, at which time every one of you . . . every last one of you in that house . . . says he was alone in his room. So nobody corroborates nobody. Every last one of you sulking in his tent like Achilles." He grinned and glanced over at me for reaction. "Told you I was no dumb *shmo*. Went to college and everything. Surprised?"

"Why should I be surprised?"

"Sure you are. Big dumb-looking guy like me, sure you're surprised. At night, of course. I mean I had to sweat for my education. Nobody hands out tennis scholarships to N.Y.U. night school."

"Horowitz—"

"But that's okay. I mean that I had to sweat for it. I learned more."

I half turned toward him. "I'll tell you what. Why don't you drop me at the next corner?"

"What for?"

"So I can get a cab."

"A cab? What for?"

"Because I'm tired of listening to the crud you've been throwing around."

There was a moment of silence. And then when I thought he was about to explode, he grinned. "Hard nose," he said.

I said nothing.

"Okay, okay, in my own way I was finding out things."

"What things?"

His grin spread. "Maybe just that you're a hard nose."

"Do me a favor. The next time you want to know something, just ask. I mean why play games?"

"All right. Who sent Mr. Cooper those threatening letters?"

"I don't know."

"Just ask, huh?"

"I *don't* know."

"Well, now, you see that's why a cop has to play games. Because if he doesn't he's likely to collect a whole slew of I-don't-know answers, which is a hell of an unproductive way to run an investigation. The fact is it was Mr. Ramirez who

55

wrote those letters. Three of them, in case you didn't know. Typewritten, in case you didn't know. Same message: 'I'm going to kill you.' All this in case you didn't know . . . which is sheer horse manure, because, of course, you did know. How can I be so sure? Because I was standing six inches away from Mr. Ramirez, this morning, when he told me he wrote the letters. And when he told me also that you had advised him to come forward with said information. So, now, look at all I've learned by playing games, Mr. Mathews. Among other things, I've learned that you will lie for Mr. Ramirez, just as you probably will for Mr. Clark. And I've learned it's unlikely that you and Mr. Ramirez *conspired* to kill Mr. Cooper. I mean, singly, you're both nice, juicy suspects, but as conspirators you don't figure. Because your lines of communication would be at least good enough for you to know he was going to spill to me this morning. How about that, Mr. Mathews?"

"I'm impressed."

"If you're not, you should be. That ain't half bad detective work. Tell me about Mr. Hazlett."

"What about him?"

"Well, he was Johnny-come-lately. He says he didn't arrive at the house until after Mr. Cooper's demise. Is that a fact?"

"I've told you so before. He got to Elinore's just before you did."

"That's right, I remember you saying so."

"And you probably remember Meg Fraser saying so, too. And Berto. And Timmy. Because we were all standing in front of the house when Chris drove up."

He smiled. "That's right, I do. So this Mr. Hazlett, in addition to having what on the face of it seems to be the only thing even resembling an alibi, missed the hair-pulling. I mean that free-for-all during which Mr. Cooper fired off all those funny lines that sent everybody scattering up to his or her room. But Mr. Hazlett wasn't the only one who missed it, was he? Miss Cronin and Mr. Clark, they missed it, too, didn't they?"

"Yes."

"Let's see now . . . Mr. Clark, he was unpacking. And Miss Cronin, she was sleeping off a bit of a jag. That right?"

"So I understand."

"They wasn't pals, was they, Mr. Clark and Mr. Cooper? Didn't Mr. Cooper just get through stompin' all over Mr. Clark in some tournament or other?"

"South Orange."

"Did Mr. Clark dislike Mr. Cooper enough to bash his head in with a rock?"

"I thought it was the base of a lamp."

"Lamp . . . rock . . . what difference does it make?"

"You never stop playing, do you?"

"*Did* Mr. Clark dislike Mr. Cooper that much?"

"Ask Mr. Clark. And now if you're going to ask me the same thing about Miss Cronin—or anyone else for that matter—save your breath. I'm not equipped to answer."

"That's not what I call cooperative, Mr. Mathews."

"Isn't it?"

"Do I get the feeling you don't care much one way or the other if we do or we don't catch Mr. Cooper's killer?"

"*Is* that the feeling you get?"

"I'm afraid so."

"Well, I won't argue with you."

"I see, I see," he said, pretending more shock than I thought he was experiencing. "So what's a smart cop like me supposed to infer from that, Mr. Mathews?"

"I'm waiting to hear."

"That maybe *you* disliked Mr. Cooper bad enough to kill him?"

"The fact is I didn't."

"Didn't what? Didn't dislike him or didn't kill him?"

I took a deep, irritated breath and kept my mouth shut.

"Do I bug you, Mr. Mathews? Do I get under your skin?"

"Yes, you do. And what's more it seems to me you waste a lot of time, which is something you were all hot and bothered about earlier."

"Uh-uh," he said, shaking his head. "I was talking about *you* wasting time. That's different. Like I read once where this great photographer gets what he wants from a subject by clicking away . . . just click-click-clicking away. I mean that's how he gets at the truth, see the parallel?"

"Vaguely."

"Only with me it's questions. The process is the same."

"If you say so."

"You mean I don't strike you as a great detective?"

I kept silent.

"How many entered in this tournament?" he asked in one of those lightning switches I was almost—not quite—becoming accustomed to.

"Why?"

"Just interested."

"I'm not sure. Maybe ninety men and fifty women, thereabouts."

"The one who wins, he's the best in the world, right?"

"In the U.S. It's the U. S. Open, so he's the U.S. champion."

"You been there, haven't you?"

"Twice. The last time four years ago."

"You and Mr. Ramirez looked pretty good out there this morning. I mean you looked like you knew what you were doing, but I guess practice is different."

"Practice is different, yes."

He paused. "Didn't notice Mr. Clark out there practicing. How come?"

"Stick around, and you will. Everybody practices. Even Timmy."

"He the favorite now?"

"Listen, Horowitz, why don't you buy yourself a news-paper."

"What I read in the newspapers is that Mr. Cooper was a major figure in the world of tennis . . . a big star . . . a very, very important man, so the cops—namely Jake Horowitz—should get busy and solve his murder in a hell of a hurry. Now when I read a thing like that, I get a little nervous. Why? Because that says heat. And to a man who's maybe looking to be captain soon heat is a thing to worry about. So don't get too smart with me. A little pertness, that I don't mind. But don't push too hard. When irritated, this Jew pushes back. So how about when I ask a question you just concentrate on answering it. Now, was Mr. Cooper the *late* favorite?"

"He was top seeded."

"Seeded? Ranked, you mean? Like who's favored to win, who's next in line and so on?"

"We're back to playing games, aren't we?"

"Why?"

"I can't believe you didn't know that, but all right, have it your way. The answer is yes."

"And seeded behind Mr. Cooper is Mr. Clark," he said softly, as if to himself, as if suddenly I wasn't there, as if it wasn't a perfectly awful piece of ham acting.

"Oh, come on, Horowitz."

"Come on where, Mr. Mathews?" he asked, six-feet-five of guilelessness.

"You can't be seriously suggesting that Timmy might have killed Cole so he could be sure of winning the tournament?"

"What do *you* think?"

"I think it's crazy. In the first place, even with Cole dead Timmy *isn't* sure of winning the tournament . . . unless, of course, he's planning a massacre."

"Would it have to include you, this massacre?"

"If he were thorough. And in the second place, sure twenty

59

thousand dollars is a respectable check, but it's ludicrous to suggest he'd murder for it."

"I knew a hit once was made for two dollars and fifty cents."

"That may be true, Horowitz, but as a pro Timmy earned damn close to a hundred thousand dollars last year."

"All right, all right, tennis players ain't like ordinary men. They have higher standards. So, why *would* Mr. Clark have murdered Mr. Cooper? Race?"

"What?"

"Race . . . black men, white men . . . Mr. Cooper was a bigot, wasn't he?"

All at once I felt very tired. I felt like a gaffed fish after thirty minutes on a clever line, all played out and ready to be reeled in. "Tell me something. What made you pick me? I mean why me to work on as opposed to all those others?"

"Instinct," he said, smiling. "It told me you'd be just right."

"Just right exactly how?"

"I didn't want anyone too dumb because that'd be worthless. Or too smart because then he'd be tricky. What I wanted was someone ordinary, like yourself."

"Thanks."

"Now, now, no offense. Ordinary's the wrong word. Representative, how's that? Yeah, that's better. Because what I needed was some zeroing in, an insight into the way you tennis cats think."

"In other words I've just delivered what amounts to an orientation lecture."

"Satisfactory job. I'll use you again."

"Terrific."

"Yeah."

"Thank God," I said, and for the first time during our dialogue managed to puzzle him. In explanation, I pointed out the funeral home. "Compared to you, even that looks good. So long, Horowitz."

I got hastily out of the car and two steps away before he called me back. "Seriously now," he said, looking serious. "A cop on a case like this, he can use all the help anybody offers."

"Can he?"

"Sure he can. And it's what good citizens are supposed to do, right? I mean a man calls himself a good citizen, he's supposed to aid, not impede, the forces of law and order."

"What kind of help?"

"Well, for starters . . . just starters, mind you . . . there's the matter of Mr. Cooper's clothes."

"What about them?"

"Where are they?"

"How the hell would I know?"

He stared at me for long enough to make me intensely uncomfortable and then he relented. "All right, maybe you don't know. Let's say I believe you. The fact is they've disappeared. The fact is the corpus was naked as a jaybird. So let's try you on this. Why?"

"What do you mean?"

"What do I mean? I mean when you kill a man and leave him jaybird naked, there's got to be a reason for it, right? So what does nakedness say to you?"

"Nothing."

"Nothing?"

"You heard me."

"Do you want to hear what it says to me?"

"No."

"I'll tell you anyway. Because if I expect to get all this help from you, I have to open my mind to you, right?"

"Don't bother."

"It says sex to me. S . . . E . . . X. Now, that's a pretty

good association, isn't it? I mean a psychiatrist wouldn't be unhappy with an association like that. Nakedness-sex."

"Terrific."

He nodded in agreement. "Now, I'll tell you what's important about that. We all know somebody hated Mr. Cooper. What's important is maybe somebody loved him, too."

With that he gunned the motor and zoomed away. At the first corner, he went through the light.

The funeral was as grotesque as I knew it would be. Things were said about Cole that underscored how hard it is for eulogy to live with truth. And how compatible ritual and mawkishness can be. They got his age and sex right. After that, it was all downhill. The mourners were not mourners, but a mixed bag of curiosity seekers and friends of Elinore. (Daddy was represented by a telegram. *His* corpus was in Brazil.) Elinore's grief was real though, and it reached out to hurt. Nevertheless, I returned to the house wearied and cynical and found Timmy waiting, smoldering, in my room.

Timmy was not one of those black men labeled so for the sake of convenience. He was emphatically black. There was no compromise in Timmy. Not in the way he looked and not in the way he confronted the world. At least the white world. For the non-white world, however, I suspected he had a whole separate set of standards. Certainly he was different with Berto than he was with me, and from that difference you could project warmth, kindliness, tolerance toward his fellow man, provided the color was right. But white was an affront to him. White goaded him like spurs, gave him no relief. Elinore was the one exception, but even with her—though I was sure he loved her—he was often abrasive, almost deliberately so. As if loving her were a weakness, a calico patch on iron clothing.

He was a big man, an inch or so taller than I, ten pounds heavier, and much more agile than one his bulk had any right to be. Seated warily on the thin edge of my bed, he looked like a nervous panther not many seconds from springing. "Did you get it all set up?" he said even before I could shut the door behind me.

I didn't know what he had in mind, but there was nothing ambiguous about his anger. As always, with Timmy, I tried to pause a beat to keep my own anger in check. This was necessary for coexistence. "Get what set up?" I asked, after that beat.

"You and the pig."

"Spell it out for me please. I'm dimwitted today. I'm bushed."

"Cole murdered; me railroaded. How's that, man?"

"It doesn't make it any clearer."

"While you were crying your eyes out at the funeral, the pig paid me a visit today."

"All right. So?"

"He said he had a long talk with you. Among other things, he said you told him that with Cole out of the way, I figured to win the tournament."

"What were some of the other things?"

"He said you told him I hated Cole."

"Anything else?"

"That's enough, man. I see the lynch mob forming."

"Crud."

"You ever seen a lynch mob, man?"

"No. Have you?"

A grin flickered up but was wiped away instantly. "No," he admitted. "But that don't mean I don't recognize the signs."

"Horowitz lied."

"Why would he?"

"Because he's a compulsive schemer. And because he doesn't give one single damn about anything but catching his murderer. And when he lied to you it looks like he accomplished exactly what he wanted to. He set us against each other. And he figures if he can do that often enough, one of us . . . you, me, anyone else he works on . . . is going to whiplash with something he can use. That's the way he operates."

"Suppose I don't buy that."

"It's the truth. Everything after that is your problem."

"Not so, man."

"Why not?"

"I mean I got a thing I could whiplash with. I mean like if I get the feeling they're hot after this black hide, I could give them another scent. And that would be your problem."

"How mine?"

"Does he know about Cole and Meg at Wimbledon? I mean if he's looking for motives, you got a fat one. Cole done took your woman."

I kept silent.

"All I want is to keep you straight," he said. "Behave yourself, and I got nothing to tell."

"Tell any goddam thing you please," I said, and went into the bathroom to wash my face.

He followed me to the door. "How come you didn't hit me? For a minute there you wanted to."

"Because you scare me to death."

"I don't scare you. No more than you scare me."

"All right, then, because all of a sudden it didn't seem very sensible. I'd hit you, you'd hit me, and we'd end by breaking up Elinore's furniture. And after it was over, I'd be ashamed of myself."

"Ashamed? Why?"

"Because I hadn't been smart enough to keep from acting like a moron."

"Hitting back, man. That can be a matter of pride."

I finished drying myself. "Listen, if you're fixated on getting someone to slug you, I'm sorry. I'm just not in the mood. Anyway, we seem to have wandered from the point. The point being that Horowitz jobbed you and will job you again. Now if you believe that, it might be helpful to you. If you don't, that's okay with me, too. But I'm interested in something. You've known me for a while. I mean we haven't just met. Do you really think I'd try to talk you into a noose?"

"You're white."

"That means I'm capable of anything?"

"It means it makes sense for me to be careful. Means if I got a club I can use, I want you to know about it. It adds incentive. For you to be good."

"Some club. If Horowitz doesn't already know about Wimbledon, I'll be shocked. Hell, I'll be shocked if he doesn't know when I was toilet trained."

"He don't look that special to me."

"Doesn't he? I think maybe he does. I think maybe that's why you're here. Listen, I don't know any secrets about you, Timmy. Honest to God I don't, if that's what's worrying you. But if there are any . . . I mean any Horowitz might be fascinated by . . . I wouldn't keep them from him. I really wouldn't."

"My life's an open book, man," he said, moving away from the door to let me by. "You see before you one innocent colored man."

"I'm going down for a nightcap. Want to join me?"

"No." He looked at me. "I'll go in and see Elinore. How was she?"

"At the funeral?"

"Yes."

"Holding up. But no more than that."

"I'll go in and see her." He glanced at me again. "There's no way I was going to that funeral. No *way*. Even for Elinore. I got principles, believe it or not."

"Why wouldn't I believe it?"

"Even a black man can have principles."

"Even a black man. Fancy that."

"And sometimes he'll stick closer to them than a white man will."

"Imagine."

"That's because we're inferior, see. We're not sophisticated enough to be hypocrites."

"Interesting. Interesting sermon. Is it over?"

"How about you, Matty? You think I killed Cole?"

"I don't think about it, not one way or the other."

"That borders on saying you think I might have."

"Might have includes a lot of people."

"Come on now, man, be honest with me. You'd put me close to the top of your list."

"If I had a list."

"You know who's at the top of mine? At the very top?"

"Me?"

"That's right," he said. He grinned glitteringly and left.

As I descended the stairs, I heard another angry voice, this time coming from the den—Dot Magruder's. And under it, Meg's, trying to calm her. Though the sound was loud enough, the words themselves were indistinct, muffled by the door. In addition to Dot and Meg, Chris was there also, but only Meg looked up as I entered. The others were too much engaged.

"He was a *man*," Dot was saying, her big fists clenched into weapons. "Maybe he wasn't any goddam saint, but he was more of a man than you. More of a man than you ever were on the best day you ever had. And I won't have you telling filthy lies about him."

Chris looked upset. "What lies, dear old girl? I—"

"Just because he's not here to protect himself, you think you can say any goddam thing you please. Well, you can't. Because I won't let you. Because if I hear any more drunken gossip out of you, I'll kick your duff the way he would have."

"All right, Dot," Meg said, "that's enough. Elinore's up there trying to get some rest."

"Then tell him to keep his dirty mouth shut."

Chris turned to me, hands outstretched. "Lad, I don't know what all the ruddy yammering's about. I swear I don't. I didn't say a ruddy word. All I said was—"

Meg moved in fast. "Chris!"

"Ah, stuff it," he said, and lunged from the room, an exit which strove to reconcile unreconcilables—dignity and a noticeable listing leeward.

"Bum!" Dot called after him. "Drunken bum!" But her voice had descended a decibel or two, and she was clearly cheered by Chris's discomfiture. "Sorry, kid," she said to Meg. "Didn't mean to cause such a ruckus, but he shouldn't have done that. I mean he had no right to speak that way about Cole. I mean he's a foreigner, after all."

Remembering an earlier scene, in this very room, just a few short days ago, I was left almost breathless. Still I managed to say, "Three cheers for patriotism."

But irony, too, was foreign to Dot. "Goddam right," she said brightly. "I can use a swim. Anybody want to join me?"

We shook our heads. She swung her own head toward us. "Cole was a man," she said, pronouncing his epitaph. "Whatever else he was or wasn't, he was a hell of a man. And I for one will never forget it." Stepping high and proud, she took her leave.

"How much of all that can you explain to me?" I asked when we were alone.

"I want a drink first," she said.

"Me, too, if you don't mind."

She made them, and I was foolishly pleased when she poured Scotch and soda for me without having to ask.

"Joe Farragut's gone," she said. "Did you know that?"

"Gone? Split?"

"Yes."

"Does Horowitz know?"

"He came here to see Joe. That's how we found out he was gone. The lieutenant is up in Ann's room now, grilling her about it."

"I'll bet he is."

"Well, I don't know what right he has to be quite so upset."

"He probably doesn't like it when his orders are taken lightly. Yes, I can see that as one of his areas of sensitivity."

"But it *wasn't* an order. He went out of his way *not* to make it an order. He merely requested that we all stay around."

"On the other hand maybe he isn't upset at all. Maybe he wanted one of us to make a break for it."

"Why?"

"He moves in mysterious ways."

"At any rate that's what started it between Dot and Chris. Chris came in and told us about Joe. He said it looked bad for Joe. And if he'd left it at that nothing would have happened. But you know how Chris is, he likes his effects. And when neither Dot nor I got terribly excited, he added that bit about Cole's having just had sex before he died."

"Say that again please."

"I thought you knew."

"How would I know?"

"The lieutenant told Chris. I thought he might have told you, too."

"What am I, his confidant?"

"I'm sorry. Why are you so annoyed?"

"Suddenly everybody seems to think I'm Horowitz's fink. Or his stooge, or whatever you want to call it."

"I don't want to call it anything at all. You asked me to tell you something, so I'm trying to tell it to you. If you've changed your mind . . . ?"

"Now who's annoyed?"

"I am, of course."

For a moment our gazes semaphored challenges, and then I drew mine to safety, to a study of my glass as still life. "We do seem to rub each other the wrong way," I said as non-abrasively as I could.

"So what else is new?"

She was poised for flight. To keep her with me, I changed the subject. "Who did he have sex with, did Chris say?"

"Not in so many words."

"I don't follow."

"That was what caused the trouble. He implied it was with Farragut."

As much as anything else it was Meg's matter-of-factness that rendered me speechless. Rain tomorrow, she might have said with the same lack of color in her voice. And while I pulled myself together, she went on. "As you saw, Dot wasn't at all happy about it."

I hesitated a moment, then plunged ahead. What the hell—if unflappability was the name of the game, two could play. "How about you? Do you think it's possible?"

"Why wouldn't it be?"

"Cole?"

"Why not Cole?"

"Was he the type?"

"What type are we talking about?"

"Womanizer."

"Well, you see I would have said seducer."

"I suppose there's a difference?"

"I think so. I think a seducer's bag is not sex nearly as much as it is . . . conquest. I mean *that's* the kick. That being the case it might not make such a sensational difference whether the object was male or female."

"I'm impressed."

"Are you?"

"Yes. You've gotten smarter."

"Thanks."

"I meant that seriously."

"All right then, really thanks. If it's true, it's no accident. It came with thinking. Anything you get a chance to do a lot of, you tend to get better at."

"Thinking about Cole?"

"Yes. And about myself."

"And about me?"

She stood up. "I want to look in on Elinore."

"No. Please don't go yet. All right, let's talk about something else. Tell me why Dot was so furious. I mean I can understand a certain amount of affront, but it seemed more than that. It seemed . . . I don't know . . . personal."

She kept silent.

"It was personal?"

"It's really none of my business. Nor yours."

"Cole had *Dot?* Dot Magruder, the iron maiden herself? My God, did he stop at anything?"

"Oh, don't be such a fool," she said, and turned away from me. But then instantly she turned back again. All at once her face seemed much older. When she spoke her voice was tightly controlled, but the bitterness was unmistakable. "Cole was a *force,* can't you understand that? I don't know what it took to set him in motion, but once that happened he was relentless. Once the object was selected . . . *whatever* the process . . . he kept coming at you and coming at you because he'd learned that if he did, he'd be there one day when you were vulnerable. And then he'd have another scalp. And anyone with any brains at all knew what he was doing, of course, but it didn't make any difference. Because by the time he got you, you were either too tired to care, or so in need of some kind of gratification—or punishment— that his lack of feeling for you was an irrelevance."

"And that's how it happened with . . . Dot?"

She looked at me. "You know I'm not talking about Dot, don't you?"

"Yes."

"Do you want me to go on with this?"

"I think so."

"Why? Because you're hoping I'll say I hated him. I didn't. I hated myself, and I hated you, but not him. He was just . . . I never felt he was human enough to hate."

"I did."

She was startled by this and, in turn, startled me by saying, "Did you kill him?"

"Do you think I could have?"

"Oh, yes," she said. "There's enough violence in you for that. But then there is in me, too. In all of us here."

"We found the body together," I reminded her.

"I know."

"I see. I could have killed him earlier and then faked finding the body. Is that what you've been thinking?"

"I could have, too. You haven't wondered the same about me?"

"No."

"Why?"

"Maybe it's because I like you better than you like me."

"And then again maybe it's because you didn't know until a moment ago that he'd had sex just before he died."

I kept silent.

"Ask me," she said.

"Ask you what?"

"Ask if it was me, not Farragut."

I winced, but then I said, "Was it you?"

"Do you think it could have been?"

I found it difficult to lift my gaze to hers because if I did, I knew she'd see I was still waiting for her answer.

"No, it wasn't," she said.

Now I could look at her.

"So what does *like* have to do with it, Matty? The thing is
. . . the dreadful thing is after three years of being married
to each other we know zilch about each other."

"Zilch?" I could not keep from smiling, which was a mistake, of course.

"It's not funny. It's the difference between us and what
happens in a good marriage. In a good marriage, you don't
have to wonder. You *know* about each other."

"Are you sure you aren't overestimating? I mean even a
good marriage takes place between humans."

Another mistake. "Well, if I am it's academic, isn't it?"

I watched her go; her back rigid and forbidding, her bottom
soft and made for my hands. She left me alone in the room
with that desolation a man feels when he badly wants a
woman who doesn't want him. Against that bleak feeling, I
decided to have another drink. I poured it for myself, then
flicked on the television set, and sat back sipping while I
watched the news. The news informed me that there were
no new developments in the Cole Cooper murder. Which,
in turn, reminded me that I had a blessing to count: a certain
diminution in journalistic intensity. Not total, still the clus-
tering of reporters that had hovered round us all in the immediate aftermath of Cole's death was manifestly less thick.
A feature writer here and there. An occasional manageable
phone call from one or another of the city desks, but temporarily, at least, we had subsided from the headlines. Now
the sports news. Here, I was informed that I stood a remark-
ably good chance of becoming the first major upset in the
tournament tomorrow. A piece of information, incidentally,
that was already part of my body of knowledge.

I flicked the set off. I began thinking about Farragut's dis-
appearance and was soon involved in a series of speculations
jumping off from this. And that was good because Meg re-
ceded a little. What made Farragut run, I wondered. Guilt?
Fear? But this implied that he and Cole *were* lovers, which

—despite Meg's analysis—was still so difficult for me to accept. But was it all that difficult for Horowitz to accept? I remembered the association he had offered me earlier in the day: nakedness-sex. "When you kill a man and leave him jaybird naked, there's got to be a reason." Had Horowitz been hinting at perversion? Had he, perhaps, hinted this to Farragut, causing him to panic and run? Certainly, you wouldn't put that kind of ploy past Horowitz. Nor was it hard to produce the unhappy image of poor Joe Farragut quivering at even a feather's worth of pressure. But it *was* hard to see Farragut as a murderer. I wondered if Horowitz really thought he might be. Maybe so, maybe not. And maybe, in his cabalistic, hugger-mugger way, he had other fish to fry.

Before I could get much beyond this, Berto came in. I told him what I'd learned, which was news to him, though he took the news as calmly as Meg had reported it.

"You think it's possible, too? About Cole and Farragut, I mean."

"*Compadre,* name me a thing that is not possible. The world is full of cabbages and kings. And queens also, my sainted grandmother used to say."

"She said that, did she?"

"Often."

"Your sainted grandmother should meet Horowitz's wise old grandfather, and maybe they both ought to confer with him. He says he can use all the help he can get."

"An interesting notion. As it is everybody thinks everybody else did it."

"So I gather. Is there a number-one seed?"

"I suppose now that must be Farragut."

"I can't see Farragut, can you?"

He took a moment before replying. "A murderer who does not run to type might still be a murderer," he said. "And yet I agree with you. I can't see Farragut."

"All right then, outside of Farragut is there a number-one seed?"

"*Sí, compadre.* I think it is you."

"Thanks."

"Timmy thinks it is you."

"He told me."

"On the other hand, Wally thinks it is Timmy. But that is because he hates blacks. He thinks all blacks are potential murderers. Chris Hazlett thinks it is me. Meg thinks it is Ann. Ann thinks it is Farragut, and Farragut, before he departed, thought it was Dot Magruder because he thinks she is a lesbian, and he thinks all lesbians are potential murderers. Our Elinore, only, is above suspicion."

"Is any of this true?"

"A little. It is true that Wally hates blacks despite all the sweet reason Elinore has tried to instill in him through the years, and it is true that Chris told me just now he is certain I sent Cole those threatening letters."

"Ah, yes, the letters. They embarrassed me this morning, your letters. You neglected to tell me you were going to make a clean breast of it to Horowitz."

"I thought about that on the way to the funeral. Forgive me, *compadre.* Was it painful?"

"It smarted. How did you explain the letters to Horowitz?"

"The truth. I told him I was given to bad jokes which nine times in ten came back to haunt me. He was understanding."

"But did he believe you?"

"Señor Horowitz keeps his own council. What do you make of him, this *teniente?*"

"I make of him one tough *hombre.*"

"Sí." Then he grinned. "I am glad to have the conscience of a baby."

I finished the last of my drink and stood. "And so to bed," I said.

"*Compadre* . . . are you worried about the Frenchman?"

"Yes."

"Do not be. Your game she is coming back. I saw the signs of this even at Merion. In your match against Cole. In the first two sets. And many more of them this morning. This morning I saw the Mathews rhythm again, which I recognized in the way one does a countryman returned from a long journey."

"Do you mean that?"

"Would I joke about so serious a thing?"

"No."

He nodded. "Then sleep well, *compadre*. Against the French, you will be Wellington tomorrow."

So I was feeling a little better as I started up the stairs, while Horowitz was coming down. "Mr. Mathews," he said, "a word with you, please."

"The name's Wellington," I said, and went on by him. It could not have been so terribly urgent, that word he wanted with me, because he didn't try to call me back.

On a sunny, though slightly breezy Opening Day at Forest Hills, I blew a beleaguered young Frenchman to hell and gone. I mean I had it all. The megagame, which is to say the mighty service behind which I could go to the net with impunity for winner after winner. Straight sets, ten aces, no double faults, to deuce only once on my serve. Not in years had I felt so dominant, so exhilaratingly like a champion, and midway through the first set I think Boucher knew what I knew, that his road to St. Helena was icy and downhill all the way. So for the spectators, it wasn't much of a match, and not many of them saw it. Admittedly, this robbed me of a tincture—not more—of my pleasure. But most of the attention was focused on the stadium court anyway, where after the Opening Day ceremonies Timmy brought truth to Germany's top-ranked player. Straight sets there, too.

Berto dropped a set and was forced to Sudden Death in

another before coming from behind to beat a scrappy, go-for-anything kid from Florida. A kid who scrambled the way Berto used to, which, by contrast, made it poignantly clear that Berto had lost half a step. A thing I'd thought before but hadn't been sure of until now. And which made me recall the day, before Cole's death, when I'd had the feeling something was bothering Berto. Watching him against the kid from Florida, I decided that what was bothering him was related closely to that half a step. Damn it, fine tennis players ought to be immortal, I told myself with the intensity of total empathy.

Dot won her match easily. So did Ann, after being sent back to the locker room by the tournament chairman to change into something less flamboyant than her Tinling see-through. Chris got slaughtered.

Over the hill as he was, Chris was still probably among the thirty best players in the world, but Alec West, a fellow Australian, was among the five best, seeded fourth in the tournament. For that kind of match-up, 6–2, 6–1, 6–0 was not an unforeseeable result. I didn't witness it. I was in the shower, but when I came out and saw Chris sitting on the locker room bench—head down, shoulders rounded, hands hanging limply between his legs—I knew it must have been bad. He described it to me, haltingly, but in vivid detail. Here, too, was a case for empathy. At one time or another in his long career, Chris Hazlett had held all four of the major championships. Not this Chris Hazlett, though. Some other Hazlett, in some other life. Involuntarily, I remembered Cole's pitiless epithet for him: Hazlett, the has-been. Then, stabbed by guilt, I reached out, touched his shoulder and, with perhaps pardonable mawkishness, said, "You'll get him next time."

He shook his head without raising it, as if it were too heavy to be supported by so slender a thing as a neck. "Not me, lad. I'm washing it up. I'll not go through the bloody shame of it ever again." He tried a smile, made it a fiasco. "Got me pride, you know."

"You've got more than that. You've got a negotiable name. You'll find a good club somewhere that needs a good teaching pro, and you'll be fine, Chris. I swear you will."

"Sure."

"Damn it, you will."

He nodded. "Might even get Sara and the kids to come back to me, once I'm settled down and all. That's why she left me, you know. Said she wasn't cut out to be a nomad. Never blamed her. Bloody awful life for a woman. But she might see it differently now, Matty. That's possible, isn't it?"

"Sure it is."

"Thanks, lad. I knew I could count on you to get the regimental colors flying." He tried another smile, and it was as ghastly as its predecessor. Because, like something amputated, he was already missing the crowds, the excitement, the cushy hotels, the champagne flights, the joy of exhibitionism, the snobbery of being special . . . all of which were part and parcel of that nomad's life so bloody awful for a woman. And so compelling for him that he had clung to it two years longer than he should have, demeaning himself dreadfully in the process. Nor was he relinquishing it now voluntarily. What we both knew, and left unsaid, was that the crushing first-round defeat had ended his last usefulness to the hard-headed tennis organization that controlled his economics. He was a contract pro who would not be offered a contract next year. Hence: no more expenses paid, no more earnings guaranteed. In effect, he was quitting to avoid being canned.

Then, suddenly, his expression changed. Hatred animated it and so energized him that he stood and slammed his fist against my open locker door. "Cooper did it to me. At Wimbledon, Matty, that's when it happened."

It had happened long before that, but there was no point in saying so.

"Destroyed my confidence, he did. You saw it. He turned me into a ruddy bowl of gruel, the filthy Teddy boy. God, to do that to a man. To show a man up that way. He deserved to die. There's a medal owed. You know that's true."

"All right now, take it easy."

"Matty, I want to tell you something. I saw something that evening—" He broke off so abruptly that I guessed, even before looking around, I would find Horowitz in the locker room entrance. I was right.

"Keep it coming, Mr. Hazlett," he said.

But Chris recovered nicely. "I saw the handwriting on the wall," he said to me. "The end of the line, Matty boy, for this old tennis bum. Nothing left for it now but to retire gracefully. Raise a glass with me later?"

I nodded.

"Good show," he said. "And now"—swinging toward Horowitz—"unless you've got something you want to ask me about, Lieutenant, I think I'll treat the bones-and-groans to a nice hot shower."

"You're a free man, Mr. Hazlett."

He left us.

"That jerk," Horowitz said. "Don't he know he could get himself killed?"

"Killed?"

"Killed? Killed?" he said, mimicking nastily. "You follow. You follow as good as I do. You're not stupid. He's stupid, but you're not."

"I'm just ordinary."

"Representative is what I said."

"Representative, sorry."

"And uncooperative."

I kept silent.

"All right," he said, "so I'll draw you pictures. He knows something, right? Don't talk because you'll only lie. Just listen for a minute. He knows something about the murder. He *saw* something. I didn't have to hear him say it now, I knew it before. And I'll tell you *what* he knows. The identity of Mr. Cooper's sex partner."

"Didn't he tell you that?"

"Like hell he did."

"Where did Farragut's name come from?"

"From me, goddamit."

"But now you don't think it *was* Farragut?"

"Think? What difference does it make what I think. Mr. Hazlett *knows*. When I told him what Mr. Cooper was up to just before he died, it took him five long seconds to remember he was supposed to register surprise. Then I threw Farragut at him to see how he'd react."

"How did he?"

"He liked it. He got kicks from it, but that don't mean it's true."

"What you're saying to me, then, is you picked Farragut's name out of the blue? Without a shred of evidence, you—"

"Evidence? Of course I got evidence."

"What kind?"

"Never mind that now. First things first. Here's what you should follow *closely*. Mr. Hazlett, he wouldn't be the first poor slob to get himself killed because he knew too much and spilled too little—to the right party, I mean."

"By the right party, you mean you."

"That's who I mean. Look, if you was a murderer . . . nothing personal . . . but if you *was* a murderer, and you began to get the feeling Mr. Hazlett was clued into certain significant information, wouldn't that make you nervous?"

"Chris in particular?"

"He's a drunk, ain't he?"

"He drinks."

"He's a lush, Mr. Mathews. And a lush is a lousy security risk."

"And yet you haven't been able to get anything out of him."

"Only a matter of time. Provided . . ."

"Provided what?"

"You're ingenuous, Mr. Mathews." He paused to smile his pleasure at the word and then continued. "Provided nobody packs him in. So you see what I'm asking you to do? I'm asking you to maybe save his life."

"How?"

"How? Here's how. Make him tell you who was in the hay with Mr. Cooper. And then you tell me. That way he's protected. No point in anybody packing him in if the cops already know what he knows."

"There's a problem."

"What's that?"

"According to you, I get to save Chris only by finking on someone else."

"On a killer. On a possible killer. That so terrible, finking on a killer?"

"Are you sure Cole's sex partner—whoever he or she was— was his killer, too? Maybe he or she was a witness, no more than that?"

"If he or she was a witness, he or she is now an accessory."

"Maybe not even a witness. Couldn't whoever it was have left just before Cole was killed?"

"That's possible. According to Doc Heller . . . he's the M.E. . . . that's just barely possible." Then he grinned wickedly. "Anything's possible. It's even possible he or she was a they."

I was silent a moment. "The feeling grows on me that you don't take Farragut seriously, that you've ruled him out."

"Hell no, I ain't ruled him out. Right now he's still among the missing. Not for long, of course. But as of right now. So as of right now, he's suspect number one. But I ain't ruled out anybody—man, woman, nor child. I'll tell you something,

Mr. Mathews. And maybe it's something you know better than I do. That Mr. Cooper, he had a sex life just chock full of interesting odds and ends."

"What do you mean, odds and ends?"

"I mean he liked the chicks, all *kinds* of chicks, and he didn't mind a *boy-chick* or two along the way either. Mr. Farragut was not an isolated case."

"Are you saying to me, definitely, there *was* something between Cole and Farragut?"

"Are you saying to me that's news to you?"

"It is."

"Tut, tut, Mr. Mathews, you didn't even suspect it?"

"Off the tennis court, I paid as little attention to Cole Cooper as I could possibly manage."

He reached into his inside jacket pocket and pulled out a small black notebook. "Paris, Hotel Briande, May 28, this year," he said.

"What about it?"

"His . . . assignation with Mr. Farragut. Assignation, nice word."

"Who told you that?"

He shook his head, smiling.

"Farragut himself?"

"Maybe. Maybe not."

"You said Farragut was not an isolated case . . ."

"Another name or two has been mentioned, yes."

"Anyone I know?"

He shook his head, smiling.

"Listen, Horowitz, if you want to tell me, okay. If you don't want to tell me that's okay, too. But don't just stand there with that canary grin on your face because it does nothing for you."

The grin remained intact. "Just by the way," he said. "Were you thinking of Wally Edmiston?"

"I wasn't thinking of anybody."

"I thought you might be thinking of Mr. Edmiston because he had kind of a crush on Mr. Cooper, didn't he?"

"Are you married, Horowitz?"

"Am I what?"

"Is that a hard question, Horowitz? Are . . . you . . . married?"

"I was. I'm not now. Got a little Horowitz, though. Why?"

"Boy? Girl?"

"Jerome, he's twelve. Why?"

"He should live and be well, Horowitz, and I'll see you later."

He laughed and let me get almost to the entrance before—with two lumbering but ground-swallowing strides—he positioned himself so that I was staring into the wall that was his chest. "I like you, Mr. Mathews," he said. "Little by little it's been sneaking up on me. You got a sense of humor. Now my *Zayde* . . . that's Yiddish for grandfather . . . he used to say show me a man with a sense of humor, and I'll show you a man of reason. And with a man of reason, he used to say, you can always do business."

"What kind of business?"

"Give me a hand with Mr. Hazlett. I wouldn't kid you, it's for his own sake."

"I'll think about it."

"Don't think about it too long. Because dead, he don't do me much good."

"You're back to playing games again, Horowitz."

"What games?"

"Panic the Sheep."

"You know what your trouble is? You got it in your mind that this murderer is a nice murderer. I mean he's not like other murderers, he's special. Outside of Mr. Cooper, he'd never hurt a fly, this murderer. And packing in Mr. Cooper, what's that after all? It's practically an act of civic virtue, right? Only you forget a few things."

"Like what?"

"In the first place, he *ain't* so nice, this murderer of yours. I mean this man or this lady took a lamp and bashed a skull in with it. Think about that for a minute. I mean forget the words and see pictures. See the arm bashing away. See the blood and brains all over the floor. Pretty?"

"No."

"And in the second place this murderer of yours he did something *ex post facto* that was really nasty. I might even stretch that and say downright dirty. Now your better bred murderer . . . I mean your really classy murderer . . . can you see him doing a thing like that?"

"You're talking about Cole's clothes?"

"That's what I'm talking about."

"Maybe there was some other reason to get rid of the clothes?"

"Now right there I'd appreciate some help. Because I confess it to you, right there I'm in one hell of a quandary. Some other reason? Like what?"

"Blood? Telltale stains of some kind? I don't know, *you're* the detective, Horowitz."

"But you see it wasn't his or her own clothes that was got rid of. That's the point, ain't it? Bloodstains on your own clothes, sure you might want to get rid of them. I mean you wouldn't want to be seen walking around the grounds with your victim's blood all over you. That makes sense. That's an honest murderer. But *your* murderer hides his *victim's* clothes. He's different. He's got statements to make. Don't ask me what exactly because I don't know yet. But maybe it was something he was afraid to say while Mr. Cooper was alive. I'll tell you something about your murderer, Mr. Mathews. I think he lacks character."

"I wish you'd stop calling him *my* murderer."

"Talk to Mr. Hazlett?"

"I'll talk to him, but I'm not making any promises."

"Talk to him now," he said, and, with that patented combination of speed and gracelessness, disappeared.

But I never did get to talk to Chris. At least not about Horowitz's business. As Chris was coming out of the shower room, Berto came into the locker room with Stu Chambers, who'd been a Davis Cupper, our vintage, but who was now a real-estate-selling dropout. He'd played against Chris, too, so the talk was reunion talk. Then Timmy came in with a few of the others, and the talk became tennis talk. Timmy had been in the press room, where all during the tournament the stadium court victors would go to be interviewed. And he told us they'd been trying to pump him about his new contract. Until recently, Timmy had been an independent pro, which is different from a contract pro, which is a difference important to tennis players, but not, I suspect, to many others. And besides it's complicated as hell. But money does fascinate us players these days, and so someone speculated that probably at least ten of us would earn over a hundred thousand dollars that year. At this, Timmy maintained a modest silence, since he was one of them. In case you are interested, I am not. Then the talk moved to the day's activities, during which someone said, as someone always does, that the courts at Forest Hills are soft, and hence you get a lower bounce than almost anywhere else in the world. And someone else said it was funny how you could pick individual faces out of the crowd, and how they seemed to be the same ones all the time. Tie-breakers were discussed thoroughly; nine-point version versus twelve points, etc. Girls were discussed thoroughly, players and non-players. And finally someone, groaning appropriately, asked if we were all aware that by the time the year ended he would have played forty-one weeks of tournament tennis, which, he said, was sheer self-imposed slavery. We agreed, tossed in our own numbers, vowed to cut down next year while knowing we wouldn't, and shortly thereafter the group broke up; all, I think, secretly relieved that for the first time in days we had managed to avoid even the mention of Cole Cooper's name. Tennis talk. By definition, I suppose, never profound, but, to me at least, seldom less than absorbing. Which is my explanation for not having noticed when Chris slipped out. Which is also why I never did ask him Horowitz's question, because that night, drunk, he drove his car off the Belt Parkway and into a telephone pole. The police reported he was doing over eighty. Others reported a bar-to-bar pilgrimage that began around three, when he left the locker room, and ended near seven when he shot out of his last parking lot. So there is no way of being sure if he knew it was Ann Cronin in the shed with Cole, or if he was just talking for effect—to use Meg's phrase—as was so often his wont.

CHAPTER 4

THE DOOMSDAY TOURNAMENT

The Doomsday Tournament—which is what the press began calling it after Chris's death—progressed from Thursday through Monday; that is, through its third round, leaving sixteen men and eight women still undoomed. Among these were all four of Elinore's tennis-playing house guests. With varying degrees of ease, we had gathered three victories each —Timmy and Dot, like royalty, without the loss of a set; Berto, in the dangerous pattern of his opening match, by inches only; Ann, two hard-fought wins and a laugher; myself, the reverse. The last one, Monday's, against the number-five seed, had scared me badly in the process. He had played so well at the outset, forcing me to my best tennis of the tournament just to stay close. But it is a game of zeniths and nadirs we deal with here, and when which comes and when which goes are not subject entirely to the laws of probability. He'd seemed indomitable. Then suddenly he was not. An umpire's call went against him; a ball took an erratic bounce at an inopportune moment; a backhand of mine—a riverboat shot I had no right to try—flew down the line and landed on the corner as if it had eyes; and all at once he wilted. His concentration was gone. The momentum had shifted. He could fling his racket petulantly, he could stop the match to demand silence from the gallery, or to move a photographer, but what he could not do was put it together again. He was beaten. He knew and I knew that his next zenith would have to come some other day. It was a big win, a stadium win. All things considered, it was as lovely a win as a man could want.

And I woke Tuesday morning still feeling the pleasure of it. A splendid morning, sunny but not hot. Checking my watch I saw it was a few minutes past nine, and a good time for an early swim. I moved briskly—Optimistic Man always moves briskly—got out of bed, into my trunks, and went downstairs. The pool was deserted. I cleaved its surface and spent the next half hour or so swimming laps or just playing. Then I pulled myself out and flung myself, belly down, on one of the mats. The sun felt marvelous, each ray seeming to contain its own minuscule cargo of buffered optimism. I began to think of coffee. As I did, I heard footsteps and glanced up to see Elinore bringing some. Optimistic Man needs only to wish.

She set the tray down on a table and began pouring for both of us while I got chairs. She smiled at me. "You look happy," she said. "I like seeing you that way."

She did not look happy. Her face was pale and her eyes were tired. She looked about as far from happy as I had ever seen her. She worried me. Optimism began oozing from me in worried droplets.

"Come on now, Elinore. *Talk* to me."

She shook her head.

"Why not?"

"There's no point in it."

"How do you know? Maybe I can help?"

"Can you bring Cole back?"

"Oh, for God's sake."

That put pink in her cheeks, angry pink. "Don't you dare take that tone to me, Matty. You hated him, I loved him. And my feeling for him is entitled to respect."

Several moments passed heavily, after which I reached for one of her hands, kissed it, and said, "I'm an idiot."

"Yes, you are," she said, but the pink faded, and she let me keep hold of her hand.

"Talk to me anyway. I'm an idiot, but I listen good."

"Oh, it's just so many things. It's Cole and trying to get used to the idea that he's not here any more. I know how difficult it is for you to understand that, but I wish there was some way to convey to you how little I liked my life before he came along to change it. It was so . . . eventless. I mean nothing ever happened to me. Day after day would go by and nothing would ever happen. Do you have any notion how painful accumulated boredom can get to be? No, of course you don't. I know you're thinking Cole was painful, too. And you're right. He was. But it was at least the pain of something happening, and oh my God, what a difference that makes. But he's not here any more. He really isn't here any more." She shook her head and looked straight at me. "How many times do you imagine I've said those words to myself over the past several days?"

"A lot."

"Do you think I believe them? I don't. I still don't." She paused. Then she withdrew her hand, rose, and walked to the edge of the pool to stand there staring fixedly into the water. I didn't like her there. She made me think of a bridge and black, not green, water swirling far below. "It's *everything*," she said. "I feel so . . . rotten. I feel as if there's a tiny cord attached to each of my nerve ends with a thousand tiny men all pulling violently in different directions. It's everything, you know? It's everything that's happened here. *Everything*. It's Cole, and poor Chris, and it's Ann . . ."

"Ann? What about Ann?"

She turned toward me. "You didn't know? I thought you knew."

"Knew what?"

"I thought Lieutenant Horowtiz had told you."

I swallowed some bile, and, along with this, some words

89

and said, instead, "*What* did you think Lieutenant Horowitz had told me?"

"That it was Ann with Cole."

"In the shack?"

She watched me, then smiled wryly. "You're relieved, aren't you? You thought it might have been Meg."

"Why would I give a damn if it was," I said, and hurried on before she could answer. "Who told Horowitz? I mean the last I knew he was trying to find out from Chris, through me. Wait. It was Farragut, wasn't it?"

"Yes."

"That was easy. One smell of Horowitz's jail, and he'd rat on his mother. All Horowitz had to do was ask and scowl a little."

"Don't despise him, Matty. He's terrified."

"Of what? He wasn't even booked. They picked him up, brought him downtown, and an hour later Horowitz turned him loose. It's obvious Horowitz doesn't think he did it."

"It's not obvious to him. He thinks the lieutenant is playing some kind of cat and mouse game with him. He thinks Lieutenant Horowitz is Machiavelli reincarnated."

"Well, that's probably true," I said, smiling briefly. Then, finally, the implications of what she'd been saying got through to me. "You mean he's here? Farragut?"

"He came last night. To beg Ann's forgiveness."

"For ratting on her?"

"Yes."

"And got it?"

"Does that surprise you so much?"

"If you're saying yes, yes. I would have expected she'd break his neck."

"Matty, you always think everyone's so simple, so one way or the other, as if every one of us could be summed up in a three- or four-word definition. And it's just not true."

"I'll take five words and sum Ann up. What's in it for me, that sums her up."

"I wish you weren't so harsh so often."

"And I wish you weren't so starry-eyed. If you weren't you might get hurt less. Elinore, for God's sake, I like Ann, but it's foolish to try to sanctify her. She is what she is."

"And I say she's more than you think she is. For instance, I heard about Ann and Cole three times—from the lieutenant and from Joe Farragut, yes, but do you know who told me first? It was Ann herself. When there was *nothing* in it for her except the need to right a wrong."

"How right a wrong?"

"By confessing it. Matty, if you could have seen how she wept."

"I'm perfectly willing to believe a flood."

"Stop that. Please stop that."

"Elinore, think. Isn't it possible she confessed just to beat someone to the punch? Ann knows you, knows what works with you because she's had years of practice. I mean maybe Chris did see her—"

"How could he have? He didn't even get here until after . . . until after Cole was dead."

"I don't know how he could have. Maybe he got here twice. Anyway that's beside the point because apparently Farragut knew, didn't he?"

She kept silent.

After a moment I went to her and put my arms around her. "Baby, baby, I'm sorry to do that to you. Honest to God, I am. But you can't go around the way you do. You've got to develop some kind of device . . . some kind of technique for protecting yourself. You're a patsy, a born victim. You go around all the time begging to be kicked in the teeth."

"I know," she said.

"It's not even fair. To the kickers, I mean. Do you understand?"

She nodded. And then she pushed away from me. "But it's all such a bother," she said. She remained with me a little longer, studying my face as if something she'd lost might be located there. Then she turned and left. I had that feeling of having failed to say something important, something magically restorative. Only I didn't know what it could be. I felt stupid. Pessimistic Man feeling stupid and miserably inadequate.

After breakfast, still with time on my hands before having to leave for my match, I wandered back to the pool, telling myself it was *not* in search of Meg. I'd seen very little of Meg since our conversation in the den. Merely a hint or a whisk of her while she turned some corner, or left some room as if cued by my entrance. I couldn't be absolutely certain she was avoiding me, but I'd have been willing to risk a sizable bet. No Meg at the pool. Dot and Wally sunning themselves. Berto and Timmy had already gone to Forest Hills.

Wally opened his good eye. It looked angry. It occurred to me then, as it had before, that Cole's death had had a marked effect on Wally's personality. Temporarily, at least, it had turned him from passive to positive. Maybe you didn't always like what he was being positive about, but wasn't that one of the patterns inherent in coming up from slavery? I mean a slave's a slave, and, by definition, docile—but if philosophically you resented that sort of thing you also had to grant a man's freedom to be a pain in the neck.

"Ann back yet?" he asked.

"I don't know. Back from where?"

"That fool detective made her go down to police headquarters first thing this morning."

This roused Dot's ire, too. She, too, opened one eye. "Hell of a thing," she said. "Ann's got to play Bernice Mac-Masters this afternoon. Bernie's one tough broad. Hell of a thing to have to go to police headquarters on the day you play Bernie MacMasters."

"Maybe the lieutenant's got some questions to ask that he thinks are more important than Ann versus Bernie MacMasters," I suggested mildly. "I know that's hard to believe . . ."

"Goddam right it's hard to believe," Dot said.

"What kind of questions?" Wally said. "You don't mean to tell me he's fool enough to think she killed Cole. She didn't kill Cole."

"Goddam right she didn't," Dot said.

"Wally, you almost sound as if you know who did."

"I got my ideas about it."

I waited to see if Dot was going to say goddam right he does, but she refrained, and so I said, "Like who?"

"Never mind," he said. "I know you think I'm dumb. You always have. Why should I just give you something else to laugh at?"

"I never said you were dumb, just misguided."

"What difference does it make if you don't say I'm dumb if that's what you think?"

An insight that shook me a little because it was sharper than I'd thought him capable of, since, for the most part, I really did think he was dumb.

"Goddam right," Dot said.

"Dot, do *you* think Timmy did it?" I said.

She was startled. "Timmy?"

"Because that's what Wally thinks."

She glanced at him, saw it was true, and said, "Goddam right I do."

I left them to each other then, but my thought was you'll never get him, baby. He's a little too rich and a little too good-looking for you. Still, I did not think this uncharitably. Magruder was a tryer. As dreadful at men as she was splendid at tennis, but a tryer nonetheless. And to tryers, always, at least a modicum of sympathy.

As I approached Ann's door, on the way to my own, it was flung open and out popped Farragut like a jack-in-the-box.

A distraught, crazy-eyed, jack-in-the-box, who flew past me, unseeingly, though his shoulder clipped mine hard enough to bump me against the wall. All the way down the stairs I heard him muttering, "They'll kill me. They really will. They'll kill me yet."

When I looked in Ann's room I saw her standing in the center of it, hands clenched, lips compressed, gaze focused furiously on the ceiling. She wore a tiny black slip, so tiny— and she so ample—you could not move your eyes from her.

"Matty, thank God, somebody sane," she said. "Come in and shut the door."

I did and said, "What's wrong?"

"Farragut, he just got through accusing *me* of killing Cole. Can you believe that? And after I was so beautiful to him last night."

"What made him say a thing like that?"

"Honey, do I know? Can I crawl inside a queer's mind and know what makes him think the things he thinks?"

"I guess not."

"I guess *not*," she said, and threw herself face down on her bed, which rucked up the tiny black slip over her flowering rump. An act of frenzied heedlessness, you might say, if you were a stranger to her. Me, I began bracing myself.

Sobbing now. "Matty, it's been such hell today. First, that crazy policeman asking me all kinds of insane questions, and then Farragut. What next? What on earth next?"

"Bernie MacMasters?" I suggested.

"Oh, God, Bernie MacMasters. I can't face her. I just can't. I'll have to default."

"That's too bad."

"Matty!"

"Well, what do you want me to say?"

"I don't want you to say anything. I want you to come over and comfort me."

"I'll comfort you from here."

A giggle. And now a sudden flip from back to front, show-ing even more heedlessness. "Matty's afraid."

I went to her closet, found a robe and threw it to her. "Put it on."

"Honey, I do declare you've turned into nothing but an old poop," she said, but did as she was told.

"The buttons, too."

"Matty!"

"Button the goddam buttons."

"I knew this would happen," she said, obeying again. "The moment I heard Meg was here I knew we wouldn't have any fun. There. Do you feel safer now? Or must I dig out my chastity belt?"

"You never had one."

"Honey, you're mad at me. I can tell. Has that bastard Farragut been lying to you, too? You mustn't listen to a thing he says."

"Mustn't I listen to Elinore either?"

"Ouch," she said, grinning. "Ouchie-wowchie. Well, that tears that, doesn't it?"

"Whatever that means."

"I'd hoped to get to you *before* Elinore."

"Why?"

The grin widened. "I wanted to sex you on to my team."

"I know. But why?"

"No particular reason," she said, shrugging. "Except a girl always needs friends, and you make a good one. Everybody knows that."

"Thanks."

"But now you're mad at me, aren't you? Because I've been bad to Elinore. Well, I couldn't help myself."

"Of course not."

"I couldn't, Matty."

"He hypnotized you."

"He *raped* me."

I laughed. "Annie, baby, come on now."

"It's true. I swear it is. I never liked Cole, you know that."

"You never slept with him either?"

"I didn't say that. A long time ago, it was different. I guess a long time ago I did like him. I mean when the four of us were growing up together. And there was some . . . experimenting. But that was ages before Cole married Elinore."

"Now say it to me again. Cole raped you?"

"Yes."

"Truly raped you?"

"Oh, all right, if you want to be stupid and technical about it, I suppose he didn't *truly* rape me. I mean after he knocked me down and tore my panties off, it would have been a little silly, wouldn't it, to have a nervous breakdown over what was bound to happen. I mean I'm on the pill and everything. What's important . . . I mean what I'm *trying* to say is I didn't go to the shack to *entice* him. I didn't even know he'd be there."

"Why did you go?"

She kept silent.

"To meet someone else?"

"Honey, I do declare you sound just like Lieutenant Horowitz."

"Is that what he asked you?"

"That and a hundred other tiresome questions, which was really too bad of him because I do have to play Bernie Mac-Masters today. Matty, will I beat her?"

"Not unless she breaks a leg."

She giggled. "You *are* terrible. You're a simply dreadful man, which is why I suppose I like you so. Are you still mad at me? Elinore isn't. She understands."

"Elinore understands everything. That's one of her problems."

"*Are* you?"

"What?"

"Mad at me?"

"Not very," I said, and with that as cue one of her hands began toying tentatively with the top button of her robe.

"What was Farragut hysterical about?" I asked quickly.

"I *told* you. I haven't the vaguest notion."

"Not the vaguest?"

"No."

"I thought you wanted me to be your friend."

"I do."

"Friends don't lie to each other, do they?"

"That was only a fib."

"Friends don't fib either."

"Oh, all right, it was some drivel about me accusing him of Cole's murder. To Lieutenant Horowitz, I mean."

"Did you?"

"Of course I did. What else was I to do once Lieutenant Horowitz began accusing me? Whose fault was it that I was at that horrid police station anyway? Farragut's. If he'd kept his big, fat, fairy's mouth shut I wouldn't have been dragged into it. Anyway, Horowitz didn't believe me. Honey, that man is just so *tough* . . . you wouldn't believe how tough he is. I could have been Magruder batting my eyes at him, that's how tough he is."

"How did Farragut know you'd been in the shack with Cole?"

"He followed me there, the fool. At least that's what he says. I didn't see him, naturally, but it must be true because he certainly did know I was there. Although he's such a liar. He really is, Matty. He really has no feeling for the truth whatever."

"Then you didn't see him when you came out of the shack?"

"No."

"But he might have been there anyway?"

"Of course he might. Lurking somewhere, which is what I

told the lieutenant. Lurking somewhere in a jealous rage. And, oh the incredible gall of the man. Accusing *me* of being jealous when it was him all the time. Because he'd been in love with Cole for years, you know. You did know that, didn't you? Queer as queer and trying to hide it from the world with me as his cover. And that was all right. I mean it used to be all right because . . . well, he *was* a meal ticket. And he did buy me a pretty trinket or two. But it's not all right any more."

"Why? Because you think he killed Cole?"

"Don't be a dum-dum, darling. Who cares who killed Cole. No, Matty honey, that man washed himself up with me because he couldn't keep his big, fat, fairy's mouth shut."

"All right, then, just as a matter of passing interest. *Do* you think Farragut might have killed Cole? That is, how enraged does he tend to get when he's in a rage?"

"Like Tinker Bell. Remember Tinker Bell in *Peter Pan?*"

"So you don't think he's a likely murderer after all."

"I didn't say that."

"Ann, has anyone ever told you that trying to follow your line of logic is like walking a maze in a blackout?"

She giggled again. "Not in so many words. But I do think the lieutenant was shooting at that."

"And after Horowitz came down off the ceiling, what did you tell him?"

"Well, it's a fairy's thing to do, isn't it? I mean who else but a fairy would strip a man naked like that. No normal man would, would he? I mean, after all, Farragut *is* a pervert. In addition to being a liar and a big mouth."

The picture of him emerging from her room a few moments ago, traumatized within an inch of his life, projected itself before me. Poor Farragut. He was out of his league, as defenseless against her as a wood nymph at bay without a harboring tree in sight. I won't say my heart went out to him, but I did feel an itch to haul her over and whack her big, white bottom good and hard. Or maybe it was a different kind of itch I felt, because she'd been watching me, and now she started to grin—a slow, wicked, triumphant grin. She got up, wafting herself toward me like a gently blown curtain. Of sheer prurience.

"Matty . . . honey sweet Matty . . . it would be such fun. Why else do you think I got Elinore to put us next to each other? Remember how much fun it always was?"

"Go to hell," I said, and ran for daylight. Behind me, I could hear her bawdy, full-throated, scale-climbing giggle. I shut the door on it. In front of me, just coming up the stairs, was Meg, and as she passed Ann's room, heading for Elinore's, hers was the fourth face on Mt. Rushmore. To himself, Fatalistic Man said gloomily, You can't win 'em all.

Unlucky at love, smashing at tennis. I smashed my way into the quarter-finals that afternoon with as little trouble as I'd had since the tournament began. Sometimes it happens that way. You make two or three fine shots early in the match and the conceit grows on you that you're superman. Sometimes, of course, a match beautifully begun can turn around, can become gall in your mouth. But this one didn't. I won going away.

Timmy finally dropped a set, but then, seemingly infuriated by this, became the Black Tornado of Forest Hills. And blew his opponent out to sea. Magruder moved remorselessly toward her grand slam, crushing a pretty young Swede whose graceful play—and tender legs—touched the gallery's heart. That was all Dot needed. She punished the pretty Swede for all she wasn't. There was anger and cruelty in this. Blame? Blame is so much more complicated.

Bernie MacMasters did not break a leg, which meant Ann did not often break her service. Only once, as a matter of fact. In the first set, whereupon Bernie broke back immediately and went on to win, 7–5. She took the second set, love. After which, Ann, reflective, said to me, "Well, I guess it's time to get serious now. A girl can put things off only so long."

"Yes," I said, missing the hell out of the point, "you're losing power on your backhand. You'll have to work on turning your shoulder more as you go into the shot."

She stared at me a moment before comprehension happened. "Don't be a dum-dum, darling. I'm not talking about tennis. I'm talking about a man."

"A man?"

"A husband, for God's sake. Fun's fun, and tennis has been lovely, but it's time to put away childish things. Matty, *honey*, I need someone to pay the bills."

I've saved the worst for last. Berto lost to Alec West, but for one set it was a spectacular, bringing the buffs to their feet again and again in appreciation of some of the fanciest shot-making of the tournament. And Berto won that first set, returning so brilliantly from 2–5 that it was possible to hope for a day full of zeniths. But Alec was six years younger —stringy tough and invincibly patient. He knew exactly how much of himself Berto had spent. So he ran him. He stretched out the points with a merciless assortment of lobs and drop shots that kept Berto in almost constant motion. He finessed Berto—until he had what he wanted, an exhausted opponent surviving on nerve. I didn't see the last set. I had to leave to get ready for my own match. I didn't have to see it. By the time I left, a young man was mopping up an old one.

Berto was waiting as I came off the court after my win and wrung my hand hard. "You are back among the giants, *compadre*," he said, grinning. "You were so good Timmy could not bear to watch." I thanked him, then asked him to send his car back with Timmy. I would drive him, I said. He nodded.

Traffic was heavy, and so we did not talk much for the first ten minutes or so. Then I heard Berto let his breath out in the kind of sigh that often marks the end of a long inner dialogue. "Well, there is still the doubles," he said.

"Which we will win, you and I," I said.

"If this broken-down ancient can stave off the onrush of senility."

"The onrush of senility has not kept us out of the quarter-finals."

"To you, *compadre*, go the thanks for that. You have been a man and a half."

"Crud."

"I wish it were. I only wish it were." He turned toward me. "Matty . . ."

"What?"

"Foolishness," he said, and turned away again.

"What is it, Berto? Something's bugging you. And has been for some time."

"It will keep."

"Damn it, no!"

"Damn it, yes!" he said, grinning. "Berto has spoken."

He did not join us for dinner that night. When I asked Timmy if he'd seen him, Timmy said he had just left him with Elinore. They were dining in her room. This was something all of us did from time to time, an exercise akin to going home to mother. As groups, tennis players and children are not gulfs apart. This is not meant pejoratively. In the first place, both are often adorable. After that, tennis, the life style, is intense, demanding, and, on occasion, demoralizing. We tend to bruise easily psychologically. And who could equal Elinore at wiping away our tears, patting our little rumps, and sending us out to play again.

"He told me we needed cheering up," Timmy said, smiling briefly. "All of us. And so he and Elinore would work on a great joke together."

"He's right. We do need cheering up. Or something."

"Or something," Timmy said, his smile going under, his voice going cold, so that I knew we had arrived at our usual cross-purposes, though I was vague as to what they were. I was in no mood for probing, however. I left him and went into dinner.

Also absent from the table were Farragut and Ann. Nobody knew where Farragut was. As for Ann, she'd be down later, Wally said, though the query had been addressed to me. From Meg, of course. Her face expressionless, of course. Absent, too, was anything resembling conversation. Dot talked, true enough—a shot by shot account of her match—but this was sheer, uncompromising monologue. Still, something was building. You could tell it from the way Wally gobbled his food, paying no attention to it, shoveling it into his mouth in tempo with his gathering anger. And you could tell from the way Timmy watched him; warily, preparing already for a hard return of a vicious service.

"So I sucked her into it, by God," Magruder said, through a heavy forkful of chocolate cake. "I knew she wanted to come down the line with her goddam backhand, so I left it open for her. And then—"

"You *wanted* him dead," Wally said, his finger menacing Timmy like a cocked revolver. "Ever since we were kids you hated him."

"Knock it off," I said. "Wally—"

"No," Timmy said. "Let him spew his poison. He's been collecting it. For a long time. If he doesn't spew, he'll choke on it. Now we wouldn't want to see Wally strangle himself before our very eyes, would we?"

Meg turned toward Magruder. "Dot, why don't you take Wally out for a breath of air."

Dot nodded and half rose to obey, but Timmy wasn't having it. "I hated him?" he said, quiet as a bayonet.

"Yes."

"How come I did?"

"You know how come."

"I want to hear it, man. I want the words."

"Wally, for God's sake, shut your mouth," I said, trying once more though I knew it wasn't going to work.

"No, sir," he said. "No more. I've been silent too long. Somebody has to speak the truth around here, and it might as well be me. You want the words, well here they are. You hated Cole because he didn't believe in the mongrelization of the races."

It was such a fat, pat phrase—and he looked so ludicrously self-righteous delivering it—that laughter was a strong temptation. I resisted. The look on Timmy's face helped. If not precisely murderous, it was at least sobering. As he leaned forward his voice was velvety, as deceptively lethal as the sleep before freezing.

"You're glad he's dead, too," he said. "How's that, Mr. Charley?"

"You're crazy."

"You telling that to me? Or you telling it to Meg? Remember this black face? Take a good look at it. It was *there* . . . through all the times he made you eat crud. All the times he rubbed your nose in it and sent you bawling to Elinore. Oh, hell, now I know why this black face has got away from you. Because you can't see too well. That's right, man. I keep forgetting you only have one eye. But you don't forget, do you? Not you. And you don't forget either who took it from you. I'm glad he's dead? Maybe so. But to me he was just another piece of white trash. Somebody hated him more personal than that. Like maybe somebody was thinking an eye for an eye. Or even bloodier. I mean maybe that's why somebody stripped him naked. Because there was supposed to be an operation. Somebody sick, somebody really sick. Only the operation never got completed. The surgery done got itself interrupted. What stopped you cutting him, Mr. Charley? Footsteps coming up the path?"

And that's when Wally moved. Caught up in Timmy's rhetoric—magnetized by it—we hadn't been watching Wally. Actually, he, too, had been overwhelmed. At first. But then, like a fighter coming off the ropes, shaking his head to clear it, he charged. I saw this too late to do a thing to forestall him. I saw him grab the bread knife from the table. I saw him swing it up as his body lunged toward Timmy's. It was such a short distance. Less than a foot, and yet Ann stopped him.

"No," she said from the threshold of the dining room. Just that, and it was enough. Her voice wasn't even loud. Clear but not loud. Maybe he would have caught himself anyway. A moot point. But the blade point was an eyelash from Timmy's throat.

"Put it down, Wally, dear," she said, continuing into the room. She reached him and took his arm. "That's a sweet boy. Now, honey, let's go take ourselves a walk and cool our funny little heads."

Dampness glistened on Timmy's face. But when he lifted the knife from the table his hand was perfectly steady. "Take it with you, baby. There might be some other dead thing out there you'd want to cut."

"You are a dum-dum," Ann said. "I declare, I don't know why I waste my time with you."

"Ah, no, Missy Ann. Did this iggorant ol' Tom go and say somepin he shouldn't have?"

"Well, you could say thanks. You really could, you know. It's only courtliness after all, which poor Elinore has tried so hard to teach you."

"Thank you, White Lady. Thank you kindly, Missy Ann, from the bottom of this wuthless black heart. Savin' my wuthless hide when you all is so grief-struck and bereaved yoself."

She watched him—the kind of half-attention you give to an excited small boy finishing up a primerish card trick. Amused, even affectionate, but essentially disinterested.

"For the young *massa*," he said. "Ain't you still grievin' for the pore young massa?"

But if Timmy couldn't reach Ann, he could still push Wally's buttons. "Uppity Nigra," he said, spinning around suddenly.

"No, no, mustn't mind," Ann said, guiding him out, her voice a dove's coo caressing his ear. "Jealousy, darling. Can't you see that Timmy is jealous? Come, honey-sweet. I'll let you hold my hand."

"Have fun out there," Timmy shouted after her. "Enjoy yourself, White Lady. God knows, you know how."

Not hurriedly at all, she kept moving—Wally docile under her urging.

"Damn you," Timmy said, though softly now because he knew she wasn't listening. "Damn you. Damn you. I never asked you for a goddam thing."

They were gone. Timmy, without a glance at us, left, too—tearing up the stairs as if someone ahead of him had to be caught and maimed. Dot, glancing at both of us, and then in the direction of the earlier exit, said, "I better follow them. She might need my help." And there was no point in disabusing her of the notion because she didn't believe it herself.

So, all at once, like a pair of surviving pawns, Meg and I loomed large on the chessboard. Too large. After a moment of awareness we became uncomfortable with each other. "Would you like more coffee?" I asked stiffly.

"No thanks."

"That was quite a scene, wasn't it?"

She nodded. "But I wonder how many times they've played it before. I mean they all seemed so familiar with their roles. And yet it scared me."

The pantry door opened, and a matronly maid popped her head in to ask Meg if she should clear away now. She had a look in her eye that told me she'd been listening, or perhaps even watching. And that she was avid for more real-life soap opera. I decided she'd had enough and moved into the den. It was news time so, out of habit, I turned on the TV and caught Horowitz predicting an imminent arrest. He was persuasive. I was almost convinced. A few minutes later I heard some idiot . . . Spud Something, Your Man About Sports . . . empurple me in prose. "Matty has it all again. The classic grace, yes . . . he never did lose that. It's the *derring-do* that's back. The bred-in-the-bone gambler's instinct that once made him so romantic and distinctive a figure on tennis courts all over the world. Somehow, that had deserted him. Somehow, it has returned. When others play it safe . . . when the odds scream for the safe return, Matty goes for the winner. And I go for Matty as my dark horse choice to . . ." I shut his big mouth for him.

"You never did like being the favorite," Meg said from the doorway.

"What I don't like is a big mouth posing as an expert."

"The truth is you're superstitious."

I didn't answer, which *is* one of the ways I confront the truth. "Drink?"

"Is there brandy?"

"Yes."

"All right."

I poured for us. We were both sitting now—Meg had the sofa, I was in the leather armchair—but we were quite as uncomfortable as we had been earlier. Minutes shuffled by like a chain gang. The drinks, which should have helped, didn't. We were two old grads at, say, a tenth reunion—with only hazy recall of the original union. Neither of us knew what to make of the other, what to expect from the other. It wasn't even that we were hostile, just ambiguous, and this fostered a silence that was as palpable as it was painful. At least for me. Actually, she didn't seem to be suffering much. In desperation, I picked up a magazine.

Instantly, Meg leaned forward. "Am I keeping you from something?"

"What do you mean?"

"Ann looked as if she were dressed to go out."

"So?

"I just thought it might be with you."

"It isn't."

"I just didn't want to be keeping you from anything, that's all."

"Listen, if you want to ask me if I've been sleeping with Ann, *ask* me. Don't horse around."

"I really couldn't care less. You are, after all, a free man."

"Well, I haven't been."

"Ever?"

"I didn't say that."

"Why should you feel you have to lie to me? A free man can do whatever he pleases."

"And a free woman, too, right?"

"Yes."

"You've had your affairs, too, right?"

She didn't answer.

"Haven't you?"

"One," she said. "It's over now. It ended badly, and I don't think I want to talk about it."

"So don't."

"I lied to him about loving him. I lied to myself, too, because I wanted to love him. He was kind."

"And understanding."

"Yes."

"And good to you, of course."

"Yes."

"Not at all like me."

"Very little."

Silence again. Idiotically, I again pretended to read. It was an impossible pretense. I glanced up. She was looking at me. She was so lovely it infuriated me. "I need some air," I said, slamming the magazine down on the table.

I heard her footsteps on the path behind me. After a while I turned. "What do you want?"

"To talk to you."

"About what?"

"Maybe we can be friends. Maybe if we tried we could be."

"Crud," I said, and started forward again.

She followed. By this time we had reached the pool. "You better go," I said. "I don't have trunks."

"You could leave on your undershorts."

"I don't plan to."

She didn't move.

"All right," I said.

She sat down on a bench and watched me peel off my clothes. I dove into the water. I swam until my muscles ached. Once, when I glanced up, I thought she had gone. But it was only to the locker room to get a towel. She handed it to me when I climbed out. I took it, dried myself, and tied it around my middle. I started back. She followed as before. Halfway up the path I suddenly stopped and turned. "Christ, how can you be so stupid. You *know* we can't be friends."

"Why not?"

"Why not, why not, like a little baby."

"Why not? Tell me."

"You know. You're not blind."

"Because you want me too much?"

I kept silent.

"Can't friends want each other?"

I stood there, trying to read her; trying to make sure she meant what the words meant. And then I heard Berto calling my name. I managed to answer. We heard him running toward us. His face was gray. "Elinore slashed her wrists," he said.

CHAPTER 5

LOVE SETS

Wednesday Berto and I lost in the quarter-finals, a miserable performance. Berto played like a sick man, and soon I caught his disease. Together, we stank up Forest Hills. In the locker room, we sat on benches and could not look at each other. But then after a while he tried to smile. "My sins are catching up with me," he said. "I'm sorry."

"Stop it."

"*Compadre*, you have got to beat Sanderson tomorrow. If you don't I'll think it was my fault, that I corrupted your game."

"I'm not worried."

But I was.

I needn't have been.

Thursday, whatever I'd lost on the doubles court was waiting for me on the singles court, and I won blithely.

Timmy beat Bobby Rudd.

Magruder beat Pamela Davis.

The three of us were in the semi-finals—Timmy against the Italian Davis Cupper Dante Agrinelli; me against Alec West, and Magruder against Sally Jo Kennedy, who did not figure to give her too many anxious moments.

I had played the Sanderson match on the stadium court, done my interview, signed some autographs, and was hurrying to the locker room when Horowitz stopped me.

"Is it important?" I asked.

"What's the rush?"

"Meg and Magruder are waiting for me. We're going to the hospital."

"How *is* Mrs. Cooper?"

"All right. She lost a lot of blood, but the doctor says she's going to make it."

"Good."

"Horowitz . . ."

"What?"

"You're standing in my way."

"Sorry," he said, but then he reached out and grabbed my arm as I started past him. "I thought she wasn't seeing anyone yet."

"She's not."

He waited.

"We're giving blood to the blood bank."

His glance was quizzical. "So she won't have to pay for it? A rich lady like that?"

"That's not the point."

"I see," he said, nodding. "A gesture."

"Yes."

"Nice, nice," he said. "A very nice idea. I congratulate you, Mr. Mathews."

"It wasn't my idea. It was Ann's."

"That's the truth?"

"Yes."

He whistled. "People. Go figure 'em out. Imagine that . . . Miss Cronin. Isn't it amazing how people are always surprising you?"

"Amazing. Horowitz, can I go?"

"Go, go. All I wanted to say is you were good today. I watched you. Slam-bang."

"Thanks."

"Mr. Mathews . . ."

I stopped, sighing.

"Is Wally Edmiston giving blood, too?"

"Yes. He went down earlier this morning, with Ann."

"How about Mr. Ramirez and Mr. Clark?"

"Berto will, I'm sure."

"But not Mr. Clark?"

"What is this, Horowitz? What's going on in that creepy cop's brain of yours?"

He smiled deprecatingly. "No, no, no, nothing like that. Just curious, is all. Why do you suppose Mr. Clark is holding out?"

"I didn't say he was. He might not even know about it. I just found out myself a little while ago."

"From Miss Cronin?"

"From Magruder. I told you, Ann went down this morning."

"That will be interesting," he said.

"What will?"

"To find out if Miss Magruder has invited Mr. Clark, and if so, if he decides to go along."

"Why?"

But he chose that moment to appear considerate. "Don't want to make you late," he said. "You go along now. We'll be seeing each other."

"Horowitz . . ."

"I'm listening."

"What do you do when you're not haunting us? I mean as far as I know not one of us saw or heard from you yesterday. It was a little scary."

He grinned. "Well, it's a big county. And sometimes even non-tennis players knock each other off, so I keep busy. Yes, yes, I do keep busy. But you shouldn't worry, Mr. Mathews."

"Shouldn't I?"

"You're still my favorites. Or rather one of you is."

"Which one, as if I didn't know."

"Right. The one I'm going to nail." His grin broadened and was not at all unpleasant. At its outset. It was only when it lingered, Cheshire-like, that you realized how carnivorous it was. "You should live and be well, Mr. Mathews," he said, waved, and departed.

I had finished showering when Berto and Timmy came into the locker room. Timmy was fuming, but Berto was angry, too, and that *was* unusual.

"What's wrong?" I asked.

"Better hurry, man," Timmy said, "Magruder's getting impatient. She's got her VW bus all cranked up and ready to go. VW for Very White."

I looked at Berto helplessly.

He was curt. "The woman's a fool," he said.

"I know that, but what has she done now?"

"Black blood ain't welcome on this crackpot pilgrimage she's cooked up," Timmy said.

Again I turned to Berto. "She didn't actually say that, did she? I know she's not bright, and I know she parrots Wally these days, but I can't believe—"

Timmy grinned mirthlessly. "Man, man, you all do stick together, don't you?"

"Berto, make him cool it. I want no trouble with him, but he'd better cool it."

"Just so, *compadre*," he said to Timmy. "You must learn who Mr. Charley is, and who he isn't." Then he smiled. "You must learn to discriminate."

Amused, Timmy subsided.

"This whole thing is so screwy," I said. "What is she, captain of the Davis Cup in charge of picking the team? If you want to go, we'll—"

"I don't," Berto said.

"Are you sure?"

"It's a crackpot notion," Timmy said.

"Why?"

"Because Magruder is a crackpot, and crackpots get crackpot notions. Didn't you know that?"

"I didn't know it amounted to natural law."

"Well, it does."

"Well, suppose I tell you it was Ann's notion?"

"*Is* that what you're telling me?"

"Yes."

"That does change it a little. Now it becomes a piece of fluff. Irrelevant, man. And Berto and me, we got no truck with irrelevance."

He was having fun with me. Gentler taunting than before Berto had stepped in, but he was still enjoying himself at my expense, and I didn't like it. "To me, it's not irrelevant. To me, it's a way to say I give a damn about you, Elinore. It's not the only way. And I'm not going to argue it's the best way. But it's the method at hand. Which makes it relevant."

And he didn't like *that*. "Elinore knows how I feel about her," he said. "Hot dogging won't make it more real to her." But his grin was gone, and I savored a small moment of triumph.

"Suit yourself," I said, and started out, stopping when Berto called my name.

"It was beautiful with Sanderson, *compadre*," he said.

"Berto, are you absolutely certain you won't come?"

He shook his head, then smiled. "Magruder, she would make us ride in the back of the bus."

I found the VW in the parking lot, and as I climbed in I tongue-lashed Magruder for thick-headed, loudmouthed insensitivity. She professed surprise, claiming a case of overreaction. I gave this a little more credence when Meg said, "Timmy did his thing."

"But Berto was boiling, too," I said.

"For Timmy's sake," she said. "He knows better than to take Dot seriously."

"Goddam right," Magruder said.

At any rate, a short time later it had all been driven from my mind by libido, that implacable goatherd. Meg had been spending every free minute at the hospital, and so I'd seen almost nothing of her since Tuesday night. Now—impetus provided by a bump in the road—my knee was making tentative yet unmistakable contact with hers. She didn't move away. So I moved closer. Then she moved away. But not instantly, I thought, while my heart thudded faster with hope. She was wearing shorts. Brown thigh. Brown knee. Brown calf. Brown thigh. Brown-white. I loosened my collar.

After yielding our blood we wondered if one of us might be allowed to visit Elinore. The cast-iron head nurse we talked to—girth, mountainous; mouth, thin—refused, snappishly. Mrs. Cooper already had a visitor. Could we wait? No, she said; a born bitch with a taste for despotism—whipping up rules to feed her appetite. She irritated me seriously. So throw us out, I said. War of eyes. She lost—a bitch is a bully in drag—and went off muttering something inaudibly insulting.

"Let's go up," I said, and started for the elevator, but Meg held Magruder back.

"You go. We'll wait. You've got her cowed, but three of us may be too much for her to take."

I grinned. "Cowed."

"Yes. Now go before she decides her image is at stake."

I made no attempt to be unobtrusive. Cow made every attempt to ignore my existence—and none to stop me. Smart girl, Meg, I thought as the elevator doors closed. I asked myself why it was only recently I'd begun to consider her in those terms. By the time the elevator reached the fourth floor I had an answer that pleased me and was at least possible. I'd gotten smarter.

Elinore's door was closed. I pushed it gently. What I saw when I had it open a crack made me shut it again instantly. What I saw was Timmy—kneeling, his head on Elinore's pillow, her hand smoothing his hair consolingly. Consolingly?

Was Timmy weeping? My God, I thought so, and got the hell away from the door and down to the far end of the corridor. From there I could watch for him to come out without too great a risk of being seen. It took ten minutes exactly. I gave him another three or four to complete his exit and then replaced him in Elinore's room. She looked tired, and a little as if she might have been crying, too, so the first thing I said was that I wouldn't stay long.

She smiled nicely and held out her arms for me to come forward and kiss her.

I did. "I ought to kick your behind," I said immediately thereafter.

"I'll never do it again," she said.

"You promise?"

"I promise."

"I ought to kick your behind anyway, just to be on the safe side. All the worry you caused us."

"And blood, too."

"Yes, and blood, too."

"That was lovely of all of you. You shouldn't have done it, and yet, when I heard about it, it made me feel so good. As if somebody loved me."

"Everybody loves you, you fool. Even Timmy, I guess, in his own exclusive way."

"It *was* you at the door. I thought it was, but I couldn't be sure."

"I thought you *were* sure, or I wouldn't have mentioned it."

"But you won't to anyone else?"

"No, *ma'am*."

"He . . . is a very private person, our Timmy, particularly about his emotions. He fakes a lot, you know. I mean he hides things desperately. It's how he protects himself, but every now and then he explodes, of course."

"Explodes?"

"What are you thinking? I don't think I like what you're thinking."

I kept silent, thinking.

"Explodes was the wrong word," she said. "I meant that he spills over. *Harmlessly.* The way you saw him just now. He was upset, you see, because he hadn't given blood and I might not understand."

"But you did understand. You always understand, right?"

"Matty . . ."

"The point is I don't care a rap about Timmy. But I care about you, and the way you always understand so much. If you tried understanding a little less, I think I'd be a touch more optimistic."

"About what?"

"About what? About whether or not you'd try to knock yourself off again, lady."

She shook her head. "That was just grandstanding."

"It was?"

"Of course it was. I mean I know now I had no intention of dying. *I* called Berto back, didn't I? If I had really wanted to die, would I have called out to Berto to come and save me? No, after he left . . . I mean after our dinner together . . . I just got to feeling so terribly, terribly sorry for myself. So full of self-pity and aloneness. I craved attention, Matty, and so I hurt myself to get it. But then I saw the blood. Real blood, not fantasy blood. *My* blood. And it suddenly occurred to me that what I was doing was dangerous, that I actually *might* die. And I didn't want to, not the least little bit. And so I screamed for Berto to come back and help me. Never again. I was terrified."

"All right."

"You do believe me?"

"Yes."

Cow opened the door, glaring. "You don't belong here."

"Oh, please," Elinore said. "Let him stay, just a few more minutes."

"Rules are rules," Cow said ingratiatingly. And then, with a smile that was pure Gothic, added, "We make them for *your* benefit. You do want to get well, don't you?"

"She'll manage it," I said. "Even with you around." Then I bent and kissed Elinore. "I didn't want to stay long anyway. Get your rest, baby. I'll be back," I added with a glance toward Cow, who was doing her Invisible Man act again.

"Good luck on Saturday," Elinore said.

"I'll need it. Alec West."

"I know. But Timmy said you were marvelous today."

"He did?"

"Of course he did."

"Well, I'll be damned. Well, all right then, he was marvelous, too."

"Good-by, you idiot."

Cow looked up at this, as if to say *her* vocabulary might have done me justice.

When I got to the lobby again Meg was waiting for me alone. I replied to her questioning about Elinore's progress and then asked, "What happened to Magruder?"

"She went back with Timmy because she wanted to mend fences. Dot's really all right, you know. She's just clumsy sometimes."

"Goddam right," I said.

Meg gave me the keys to the VW, and we went to the parking lot to get it. It was about seven now, a soft, cool, September evening. I suddenly felt very young, light-hearted and feckless. I felt untied. And I also felt hungry. "Let's play hookey," I said. "Have dinner out."

"Where?"

"I don't know. Let's just drive."

"Yes. Let's."

Then I added, "Someplace where there's music."

We drove, we found a place, we ate, and we danced. Dancing was strange. I mean it wasn't strange, which was what made it so. Holding her in my arms for the first time in three years, I had expected to feel awkward, tense. I didn't. It was as if my body had stored hers in its memory bank—structure and texture on a set of perforated cards. Neither of us spoke much. It was nice, very nice.

We were in the bus again. Evening had shifted into night, and with this, a fierce shift in the day's mood. Happening swiftly, catching us on a country road, still thirty minutes or so from Elinore's house. Black now, starless, strong winds warning of imminent rain. And then it came, the rain so heavy that within minutes the rutted, leaf-strewn road was slick and in puddles. The wipers, flailing desperately, were unable to cope.

"Can't see too well," I said. "I better pull over."

It took a little while to find a shoulder area wide enough, but I did finally and nosed the bus into it, cutting the motor just as lightning ripped the sky into jagged halves. We braced for the thunder. Even so, the rolling, thudding power of it took us by surprise.

Once, in Italy, early in our marriage, a thunderstorm had frightened Meg into near hysteria. Only that once, but when I looked at her now I saw that her fists were clenched. She shook her head. "I'm all right," she said. I put my arms around her, and after a moment, after the briefest of hesitations—as if in a last seizure of wariness—she moved closer, nestling. Cause and effect, I kissed her.

"Yes," she said, when we were apart.

"Yes what?"

"It's the way I remember it."

"Is that good?"

She lifted her face again.

Then she moved away. Then, dressed in darkness, she did things to her clothes that were mysterious. And almost painfully exciting. When she returned to me, her back against my chest, I knew in gratitude what she had done. I touched as much of her as I could touch. I kissed as much of her as I could kiss.

"Oh, my," she said, shuddering. And we climbed to the rear of the bus and didn't give a damn about lightning or thunder or anything else that was not thrust and catch.

Sometime after us, the rain stopped. I commented on this. Her head was pillowed on my arm. She turned it in so that she could kiss my shoulder. "You . . . are . . . right," she said, punctuating with heavy breaths. "You . . . are . . . right . . . as . . . rain."

"You're tickling," I said, pulling her head back.

"Don't you like it when I do that?"

"It tickles."

"Don't you like being tickled?"

"No."

"Why?"

"It's like being tortured."

"Don't you like being tortured?"

"No."

"Not even there?"

"No," I said, clenching my teeth.

"Such a liar."

I kept silent.

"My goodness," she said. "You *love* being tickled there. You positively *love* it. Say so, or I'll stop."

"Say what?"

"That you love it."

"I love it."

"Say uncle."

"Uncle, aunt, sister, brother . . ."

"Say this torture is exquisite."

"It's exquisite."

"It is," she said, and pulled herself over on top of me.

Some time later she informed me that your average VW bus floor was very hard on your average sensitive skin, and consequently she was getting up. "I have several interesting bruises," she added.

"So do I."

"I'm not complaining, you understand."

"I understand."

Her hand touched my face. "Are you?"

"God, no."

"Better not. Complaints are torturable offenses. I seem to have lost my blouse."

"It's on the front seat."

"Stop that."

"Why?"

"Because it's late. We have to go. Now, stop it, darling, please."

"Say uncle."

"Uncle."

"Aunt."

"Aunt."

"I love you."

She pulled away from me sharply, so suddenly that I was startled into letting her go. "Now none of that," she said. She tried to say it lightly, but it came out wrong. Or maybe right. Anyway it was clear she meant it.

"What's the matter?" I asked.

"That is not the note I want this relationship to strike."

"I still don't understand. What note?"

"A serious note."

"Why not? I feel serious."

"We better go," she said, and huddled away from me on the far side of the front seat.

After a moment I set about getting myself together, and the bus on the road again. She'd been silent all that while, but finally she said, "I'm sorry, Matty. I didn't mean to get so intense. It's just that I don't want us to be talking about love. That's not what this is all about."

"It isn't?"

"No. We've tried love, and it doesn't work for us."

"I see."

She got up on her knees and turned toward me. "Listen, all this is my fault. I knew I should have arranged to be away while you were here, but Elinore sweet-talked me out of it. I'm not blaming her either, you understand. Only me. Because I knew something like this would happen. I knew I'd see you and I'd want you, just as I always have. And I knew that if you still wanted me, I wouldn't be strong enough to walk away from you. But that's sex. That's all that is, and that's where it has to stop. And if you say to me it can't stop there, then I pack my bags and leave tomorrow."

"And suppose I say to you that I love you."

"I pack my bags and leave tomorrow."

"Would you mind making that just a little clearer to me? I mean how it starts the motor for all that wanderlust."

"Take me seriously, Matty."

"I'm trying to. You don't make it easy."

"It's as easy as this. I spent some of the rottenest years of my life married to you because I loved you so much there wasn't anybody else alive except you. There wasn't even me. That's bad for a person, my dear."

"Does it have to be?"

"Yes."

"No, think about it for a minute. What made it so bad was me, wasn't it?"

"Both of us."

"It was me, mostly. Let's not argue about that because we both know it's true. But suppose I've changed."

"Have you?"

"I think so."

She waited a beat and then hit me with it. "Would you give up tennis?"

When I stopped the car in front of the house she tried to get out right away. From the way she moved, I could tell how tightly strung she was. And when she didn't say good night, I thought it might be because she was close to crying. I held her arm. "Wait," I said.

She shook her head and tried to pull free, but I wouldn't let her. "You're not going to do anything silly, are you?"

"Like what?"

"Like leave tomorrow?"

She didn't answer.

"Promise you won't?"

She didn't answer.

"Meg, for God's sake, I have to think about it. Don't I even get a chance to think about it?"

And then she broke. The tears and harsh sobs came spilling out, like live things too long pent up. Even then, she tried to force them back. "I don't like myself. Oh, I don't like myself at all. I stink," she said, and tore herself from my grasp. She fought the door, got it open, and ran up the stairs. Feeling loss literally—as if at the siphoning off of some vital fluid— I watched her go. And then I thought . . . yes, I really did . . . thank God, I don't have to play Alec West tomorrow.

But that night I lay in bed trying to construe tennis analytically; that is in terms of what it meant to me, why I was so drawn to it. I don't have that kind of mind, of course, so I made a hash of it. But I tried. At least I tried. I came up with something like this:

There were a variety of peripheral reasons for its pull—the money that had gotten big recently, the applause and acclaim, the *haut monde* life style integral to tournament-hopping. These were parts of it. No point in denying that. Appealing to us all. As appealing to me as they had been to Chris Hazlett. Less peripheral was the competition. I enjoyed its purity . . . the arena feel of it . . . a pair of gladiatorial throwbacks matching hard-earned skills. And I acknowledged that it was perhaps more important to me than it was to the general run of men to be able to demonstrate clear-cut, uncomplicated superiority. I didn't delight in acknowledging that. I was a little nervous about its implications, but there it was, and no point in being dishonest about that either. But above all, I thought, there was the basic joy you could derive from your body when it did well those things you had trained it to do. The grace and power you could generate. The sheer sensuality of laying racket to ball with maximum efficiency . . . and the way it looked, too, when the ball shot away low and hard, clearing the net by invisible inches. A beautiful hit, someone would say. And it was beautiful. Literally beautiful. The aesthetics of trajectory. True, I could yield the peripherals and retain the basics, which is what Meg was asking. Theoretically, I could do this, but on that day, obviously, my joy in tennis would be diminished. Earning my living from it gave tennis its seriousness. Its seriousness contributed to my pleasure. A weekend player was by definition a hobbyist. And who would willingly become a hobbyist when he could be serious? On the other hand, who would willingly give up the woman he loved for the sake of a game? I spent a lot of time that night denting and turning pillows, and when I awoke it was to find myself unrefreshed as well as unresolved.

It was around nine when I woke; early, but not early enough. She was gone. I had known she would be. Halfheartedly, I asked around to see if she had left any kind of message for me. She hadn't. I had guessed that, too. And yet—perhaps strengthened by this very lack—I was unshakably convinced that she would return, that she had merely gone off somewhere to be by herself, to sort things out. I say unshakably, knowing the word applies only in a part-time sense. *Sometimes* my conviction was unshakable. Other times it oscillated a little. Noon was struck, for instance, before I could nerve myself to go to her room for fear I might not find her clothes there. They *were* there, however. I let my breath out heavily, which was when I knew I'd been holding it.

I lolled around the pool most of the morning and then, after lunch, Berto and I went down to the hospital to see Elinore. No sign of Cow, but Horowitz was there. Not wanting to overtax Elinore, I'd sent Berto up first, while I waited in the lobby. After I'd been there five minutes or so I saw Horowitz come out of the elevator. He saw me, too, smiled, and plodded over to the next chair.

"She looks good, Mrs. Cooper," he said. "Color in her cheeks."

"I'm glad."

"A nice lady."

"Yes."

He crossed one heavy leg over the other, yawned, and then stroked his chin slowly, an elaborate simulation to indicate that the thought he was about to express would be casual. I prepared myself for an expressed thought that would be anything but casual.

"For a while there, I used to wonder why such a nice lady, who loved her husband . . . she *did* love her husband, didn't she?"

"Yes."

"I mean you didn't, but she did, right?"

"Move with it, Horowitz."

"Well, I used to wonder why she wasn't more interested in finding out who killed Mr. Cooper. But I finally figured it out. You want to hear?"

"Tell me."

"That I.D. is already in her possession. I mean that lady knows who put out Mr. Cooper's light."

I kept silent.

"You're not surprised?"

"Not really."

"How come?"

"I'm not sure. I guess subconsciously I wondered the same way you did. And I guess, subconsciously, that was my answer."

"You might have made a cop," he said.

I was startled. "What?"

"Now I don't say positively, mind you. I wouldn't want to be held to it, but the instincts are right. I pride myself I got a sure eye for the instincts. And when the instincts are right, it gives you something to build on."

"Well, you'd never have made a tennis player, Horowitz. Not with all that lard on your rump."

He threw back his head and roared, causing two nurses and an intern type to glance his way sharply, sensibilities clearly outraged. They were ignored for their pains. In his own good time he allowed his gusto to trickle into chuckles, and, shaking his head, said, "I like you, Mr. Mathews. Son of a gun, you do grow on a man." And then, the laughter banished to another country—as swiftly as if it had been traitorous—he said, "Which is a lucky thing for you. Because if I didn't like you . . . I mean if I didn't have a certain conception of you . . . you might be in serious trouble right now. Yes, sir, in serious trouble."

"What serious trouble?"

"There seems to be a letter. Make that note."

"What kind of a note?"

"Maybe an incriminating note . . . maybe. No signature, but somebody says you wrote it."

"How incriminating? And who says I wrote it? And who is it to?"

He shook his head.

"Goddamit, Horowitz, you toss a bombshell and then clam up? What kind of crud is that?"

"A police officer protects his sources," he said self-righteously.

"All right, protect your sources. What was in the note?"

"Motivation maybe."

"What kind of motivation?"

"For murder maybe. That kind. I don't say positively, mind you, but it's interesting. Interesting, it is. It's a love note to Miss Cronin."

"Show it to me. Maybe I can recognize the handwriting." He shook his head again.

"Beautiful," I said grimly. "Just beautiful."

"Well, don't worry about it."

I studied him. "Horowitz, you take my breath away. A moment ago I would have sworn you were about to arrest me."

"Just prodding you a little. Just trying to make sure."

"Of what?"

"That it wasn't your note. Could have been, mind you, but I didn't think it was. Still, I thought if I prodded you a little maybe I could make sure."

"And did you?"

"Reasonably."

"How?"

"It wasn't handwritten." Then he said, "Watch yourself. I think maybe you got an enemy."

"How can I watch myself if you won't tell me who he is? Or she is?"

He smiled. "See? Instincts. Like a good cop you don't leap to conclusions."

"Are you sure you don't want to show it to me?"

"What for?"

"Maybe I *can* figure out whose it is?"

"And if you did, you'd tell me?"

I made the mistake of hesitating.

"You should live and be well, Mr. Mathews, and besides I think I already figured it out." Debonairly, he touched his hand to his forehead, flicking me a salute. Then, stepping back, he left me agog with a brisk farewell bow.

Elinore did look much better. And her voice, welcoming me, was obviously stronger. While I was there her doctor came in, and she demonstrated still another sign of a recuperation progressing speedily. She demanded to be sent home. In another day or so, he promised. After he left—as offhandedly as I could—I asked if she had heard from Meg. She hadn't, she said, and then asked why in a way that indicated I hadn't fooled her. But when I answered evasively she didn't press me. I stayed about half an hour or so and then departed, resisting the temptation to ask her if Horowitz had mentioned his mysterious note.

I collected Berto, and we left the hospital. On the way back to the house I brought him up to date. He wondered if the note might be another of Horowitz's ploys. I hadn't considered that and acknowledged that it might be. But somehow I didn't think so. However, I was damned if I was going to let it bother me one way or another. If Horowitz wanted to spin webs, let him. Just now I had enough to worry about in my own parlor. An early dinner. Early to bed, too. My thoughts divided between love and war, between Meg and Alec West.

It's accurate, I suppose, to say I beat Alec in the semifinals, in straight sets, and that's the way it went into the record books. But the truth is he beat himself. Conceive of Pinocchio with an oaken racket, that's how Alec played. In one of those total and inexplicable reversals of form that reveals big-time tennis as an arrant bitch-goddess, he double-faulted incessantly, erred all over the back court, missed fat kills at the net he would see in his dreams. He was a disaster. In the third set, as we passed each other while changing courts at 3–0, I saw that he was crying. Openly, in self-hatred. I felt a pang of sympathy for him, and this scared me. Scared the hell out of me. Beat his brains in, I told myself furiously, this match could turn around. But the Blue Fairy didn't show for Pinocchio that day. Alec was so bad there was no way in the world I could tell if I'd been any good or not.

Timmy had a bad day, too. For him. He got eliminated in the doubles. Before that, against Agrinelli, for one set, he'd had the upset-conscious Forest Hills gallery in a state of galloping ambivalence. The buffs wanted the upset. At the same time, they wanted Timmy in the finals. I understood how the gallery felt. I felt the same way. Because, you see, I knew it would be easier to beat Dante than Timmy, and to someone who wanted to be champion as much as I did, the upset had serious appeal. But I'm only part coward. Hence, the ambivalence. At any rate, Timmy resolved the matter neatly. From 1–6, he came clawing back to take three consecutive sets— annihilating one opponent and chastening his next.

Magruder won.

Berto and I rode back to Elinore's together and did not talk much about tennis. With two close friends in it, I knew he had his own mixed feelings about the finals as well as a certain amount of still unreconciled pain having to do with not being in it himself. It lingers, that kind of pain. He congratulated me warmly. I allowed that and then changed the subject. I asked him if he thought Timmy and Ann had ever had a thing going.

"That is their business. And by a thing, do you mean a thing such as *you* and Ann and Ann and others had going? I tell you true, I do not like the feeling of clouds gathering around Timmy's head."

His reaction startled me. I'd asked the question without worrying overly about its implications, asked it as a friend asks, when the frame of reference is long-established mutual trust. "I'm sorry," I said. "I wasn't planning to call the cops."

After a moment he said, "I had better watch myself. I grow crustier and crustier these days. If I am not careful, *compadre*,

I will become the complete . . . what is the word, it starts
with mis."

"Misanthrope?"

"That very one."

"Is it just the tennis?"

He didn't answer.

"It's more, isn't it?"

"Somewhat," he said.

"If you've got something on your mind—"

"It's not my mind, *compadre*. Or, at least that is not where
it starts."

"It's physical?"

He smiled. "Enough of Twenty Questions. I will tell you
after the finals tomorrow."

"What is it, your health, Berto?"

"Tomorrow." And then it was his turn to change the subject by returning to an earlier one. "Yes, Timmy had a thing
with Ann. A warm thing. That is almost all I can say about
it, except that it's over now. About some matters, Timmy
talks very little, even to me. He is a hard man with an extra
word."

"Like some others I know."

"Tomorrow. I promise."

"All right." A thought struck me. "If it *was* Timmy who
wrote that note . . . all right, all right, just suppose it was
. . . could he have used your typewriter?"

"Everybody has used my typewriter. It's the touring pro's
typewriter, you know that. Why?"

"Because Horowitz said the note wasn't handwritten. And
then he said he thought he knew whose it was. And, you
know, he has those notes to Cole typed on your machine."

"So?"

"Listen, all I'm saying is if Timmy wrote a love note to Ann
Cronin he ought to hurry up and tell Horowitz that."

"You think so?"

131

"You're damn right I think so. I think information volunteered to Horowitz is always better than information he's forced to dig out himself. It's an impression that's grown on me. I mean a love note to Ann is only significant if someone's been trying to keep from Horowitz that he was in love with Ann. Or so it seems to me. Do you see what I mean?"

"Yes."

"Why not whisper that in Timmy's ear?"

"You do not *know* it was Timmy who wrote it."

"Whisper it just the same and see what happens."

He looked unconvinced.

"All right, think about it anyway. For his sake, Berto."

"I will think about it."

I braced myself for probable disappointment and then let fly. "You didn't happen to see Meg lurking anywhere around the gallery today, did you?"

"No, *compadre.*"

My "enemy" paid a visit to my room that evening. It was shortly after dinner, and I was stretched out on my bed thinking a series of not very optimistic thoughts concerning my tactics for tomorrow. First, as dispassionately as I could, I compared asset lists. It came out this way. I was quicker than Timmy. He was younger and more durable—so that toward the end of a long match the fatigue factor would be operating in his favor. I had the slightly better backhand; he, the far better forehand. Services: equal in velocity; to him, despite improvement, the edge in consistency. We were both strong all-around volleyers, both die-hard competitors. Dispassionately, he had more assets than I.

Next, I tried to recall in detail how I had beaten him the last time I had beaten him, which was some two years ago when he had been eminently more beatable than he was now. Mostly, it had been on his errors. That was discouraging. I did not think I could work his errors into my game plan. Finally, I decided that my plan must be to achieve an early lead and cling to it. My *modus operandi* would be un-relenting pressure on his backhand, which was a nice idea because Timmy's backhand *was* a shade less menacing than his murderous top spin forehand. As a plan, its basic flaw derived from the fact that Timmy would have a conflicting plan. I shrugged. If I could get my first serve in hard and deep, go to the net behind it, angle him off balance so that he, no more than I, could shape the match, I would give him trouble. If not, he'd demolish me. The odds were he'd de-molish me.

Never having been much good at the kind of self-delusion required for psyching oneself up, I tried to be philosophical about the probabilities of tomorrow. I tried to tell myself that *sharing* in the finals was a remarkable accomplishment, considering the outlook at the outset. I tried to tell myself that losing to Timmy, perhaps the best in the world, was hardly an occasion of shame. But being philosophical about losing was another discipline I'd never been very good at. I hated losing. Suddenly, I hated the thought of losing so much I simply could no longer lie there, inertly contemplating it. So I was up and pacing when the reticent, almost reluctant knock came at my door.

My enemy, Farragut—his eyes averted, his hands clasped at his chest—stood just outside looking like a willowy Judas. It was this graphic penitency that now confirmed what I had somehow suspected from the moment Horowitz had men-tioned the note. Farragut was my enemy . . . such an enemy . . . and he was here to confess.

"Come in," I said.

He hesitated.

"Come in, come in, I won't hurt you."

"You say that, but you might change your mind when you hear what I have to tell you."

"Sit down," I said, pointing to the chair. I shut the door

133

and got back on the bed, thumping up a pillow to support my head. "All right, lay it on me."

Still unable to meet my eyes, his glance was now riveted on the floor. Instead of speaking, he cracked his knuckles.

"Farragut . . ."

"I don't know where to begin," he said.

"I know about the note," I said. "Horowitz wouldn't show it to me, but he told me about it."

"Oh, God," he said. "I'm such a coward. Such an appalling coward. Can you really bear to be in the same room with me?"

"I can bear it."

"I was terrified, simply terrified."

"Okay, you were terrified. I understand that. But why pick on me?"

"You *don't* understand. *You* couldn't understand because you're brave. Only cowards understand cowards. I could never explain it to you. Never."

"Try."

He cracked his knuckles again. His glance, touching me briefly, fled instantly, as if I were naked. "I can't," he said.

"Yes, you can, Farragut. That's what you came here for, isn't it?"

He nodded.

"All right, consider that the worst is over."

"You say that, but—"

"Damn it, Farragut, you've got ten seconds. If you don't start talking in ten seconds out you go. And please, for God's sake, don't crack your knuckles again."

He did it anyway. He couldn't help himself. But this time it got him launched. "I've been arrested twice on morals charges. Did you know that, Matty?"

"No."

"Well, I have."

"So?"

"So? So?" His voice rose to only little less than a scream

before he caught it and brought it down again. "I knew you'd never understand. The second time was last year, right here in Nassau County."

"Does Horowitz know?"

"Why else is it important? Of course he knows. He's a fiend, that man. He knows *everything*. So don't you see, when Cole was found nude that way I was certain the police would start looking for me. They hate homosexuals. Everybody hates homosexuals, but the police, passionately. I'm nervous, Matty. I'm a very high-strung, intense individual and have been since childhood. And all I could think of was this awful, Kafkaesque thing happening to me. I'd be arrested, I'd go to jail, nobody would believe I was innocent, I'd be electrocuted. So I ran away."

"The note, Farragut. What was in it?"

"And then they caught me, those brutes. They came after me and caught me and threw me in a cell. I was certain I'd never see the light of day again, absolutely certain of it."

"Crud. All you had to do was sing your little song."

"That's not why they let me go. They let me go so they could watch me. So that man Horowitz could have his people watching me constantly. They know how nervous I am, and they hoped I'd panic and do something hysterical, something they could use to frame me for Cole's murder. Because they *hate* homosexuals, they really do, and, Matty, I couldn't stand it. I just couldn't. I had to get them off my back. So, God forgive me, I tried to give them you."

"Yes. So I gathered. But *why* me?"

"Here," he said, reaching into his pocket to withdraw a multifolded, dog-eared piece of paper. He handed it to me. "It's a photo-copy."

I smoothed it open, recognizing the distinctively shopworn typescript of Berto's quarter-century-old machine. This is what I read:

Too damn hot in Dallas tonight, my
Ann-gel, and it will be too damn hot
tomorrow—too damn hot for tennis.
For your sake, I'm glad you decided to
stay out of this tournament, though I
miss you like hell. Miss
your eyes and your hair and your lips
and your legs and your ten toes and
every other sweet part of you. In my
thoughts I kiss them all. The semis
tomorrow, the finals the day after . . .
in two days or less I'll hold you in my
arms again. All are well here. Berto
sends his love.

"So you see?" he said, when I returned it to him.

"I don't see a damn thing. In the first place, why did it
have to be me who wrote it?"

"I admit I leaped to a conclusion."

"Oh? You admit that, do you?" .

"I was desperate. I already told you I was desperate, Matty.
But then it does speak of that tournament in Dallas when
it was so beastly hot two years ago, and when you were in
the semi-finals."

"So were Berto and Timmy. And Wally as I recall."

"Would Wally be sending Berto's love? Of course what I
didn't stop to think of was Timmy."

"Because he's black?" I taunted him.

"Well, maybe. I'm not ashamed of my prejudices. When
you're a homosexual, you're allowed some. As compensation.
But I think it wasn't Timmy's blackness as much as it is that
Ann's white and such a bitch. At any rate, what I didn't know
then and what I know now is Timmy's been in love with her
for years."

"You have an unimpeachable source for that?"

"Horowitz."

"How does *he* know?"

"How do I know how he knows? But he does. He knows everything. About all of us . . . *the* most intimate details. Everything, everything . . . our secret shames and fantasies, our family trees, our blood types, for goodness sake. The man's a devil."

"All right, now, calm down."

"I can't. I'm sorry. Just thinking of him makes my heart flutter."

"Then think of something else."

"What?"

"I don't know. Think of why you thought the note meant I killed Cole. That's what you told Horowitz, isn't it?"

"Yes."

"Tell *me*."

"It's obvious."

"Tell me anyway. It'll keep your mind occupied."

"Jealousy, of course. Cole had already taken one woman away from you, and now he was about to do it again. I saw them meet, you know . . . Cole and Ann."

"That's right, you were lurking in the bushes."

"I was not lurking. I happened to be out walking."

"Ann says you were spying on her."

"Ann is a bitch. A bitch. A slut. And a congenital liar."

"Were you still lurking . . . or whatever it was you were doing . . . when she came out?"

"No. I left. I was furious."

"Furious?"

"Of course I was furious. I thought she'd gone there to meet Cole."

"But now you don't?"

"No."

"Who *did* she go there to meet?"

"Timmy."

137

"Oh?"

"At least that's what that devil thinks."

"Horowitz?"

"Yes."

"Did he say so?"

"He didn't have to. In the most awful kind of way I'm tuned into him now. He asked questions, you see. Terrible, probing, penetrating questions . . . and it was clear that he had Timmy in mind. Oh, yes, that was very clear. He thinks Timmy wrote that note. He thinks Timmy killed Cole. Poor Timmy."

"How'd you get the note anyway?"

"I stole it."

"That's lovely. You really are a lovely man, Farragut."

"Ann and I are *always* stealing from each other. She steals money from me. I steal things from her blackmail file."

"Ann has a blackmail file?"

"Didn't you know?"

"No, I didn't."

"She has a commitment to never being poor again. A commitment? It's a commandment . . . her own personal commandment, replacing our Creator's about adultery. She knows she's never going to be good enough to make it big in tennis, so for some time now she's been collecting things she might turn into money. That's if she doesn't get herself a rich husband."

"I see."

"Matty . . ."

"What?"

"Try not to hate me. I mean, yes I'm rotten, but didn't it take *some* courage, at least, to come here and confess?"

"Courage?"

"Can't we call it courage? I mean we both know it was mostly guilt, but maybe there was a tincture of courage mixed in with it. Can't we say so."

"All right, let's say so."

"You're a good man, Matty."

"Crud."

"No, I mean it. There's a core of decency in you, which sometimes you pretend doesn't exist, but it does. Even that fiend, Horowitz, knows it. He was funny. I mean I tried to give him you, and he didn't want you. In the worst way, he wanted somebody else. *Anybody* else except you. I decided it was his one redeeming feature. Good luck tomorrow. You'll need it, of course. But then Timmy will, too. Afterward."

"Afterward?"

"He's who Horowitz wants."

A few minutes later he left. Considering my own fail-safe attempts to read Horowitz, I wondered if Farragut was right. *Was* Timmy Horowitz's candidate? I found myself hoping he wasn't, and, in the process, realizing that I liked Timmy more than I thought I did. I wondered about the note, too. There was something odd about it, something that stuck in the crevices of my subconscious like food in a tooth and refused to be dislodged. From all this, I suppose it was an easy jump to where I went next, and yet, having made it, I was a little surprised—and not really happy—at being there. That is, I found myself trying to construe the note so that it might make sense for *Wally* to have sent Berto's love. I couldn't come up with anything satisfactory, but I kept trying. Unfair, I told myself. It's like rigging an election for your *own* favorite candidate, I told myself. And kept trying. So much for that core of decency.

I was asleep. I was dreaming. In my dream, I stood, Zeuslike, at the top of a mountain, joyously hammering thunderbolts that Timmy, diminutive, at the foot of the mountain, could not return. Unfair, he kept screaming as one after another of them tore fiery holes in his racket. The holes sealed themselves instantly, but it was clear Timmy was fighting a delaying action. "Change courts," he howled at some unseen umpire, and then suddenly he was gone. In his place was Meg. And in place of a tennis racket I held a huge ladle with which I was emptying a small bucket. The liquid poured down the mountain, a rich, creamy substance forming a neat, arrowlike path. "I'm cold," she said, surprising me because it was so obvious a *non sequitur*. "Move over and let me in."

I opened my eyes, just as she was taking matters into her own hands. With her backside as lever, she was earning room for herself in my bed, while making a whole series of exaggerated noises to dramatize how close she was to death by freezing. Which was ridiculous, since the room temperature could not have been less than seventy-five. Sleepily, I pointed this out to her.

"But I don't have any clothes on," she said. "In case you hadn't noticed."

"I noticed," I said, less sleepy now.

"Yes."

"Yes what?"

"I noticed you noticing. You have an interesting way of noticing."

"Do I?"

"It gets more and more interesting as things go along, doesn't it?"

"It does, doesn't it?"

"How would you describe your interest now?"

"Avid."

Her arms went tightly around me, her fingernails digging into both shoulder blades. "Say it," she demanded.

"I love you?"

"*Say* it. Don't ask it."

"You won't run away?"

"If I tried, you could keep me here, couldn't you?"

"Yes."

"If you wanted to be cruel, you could pin me here. Pin me to this bed like a butterfly, couldn't you?"

"I could do that, yes."

"So what have you got to lose?"

"Nothing. I love you."

"Again."

"I love you."

"Once more."

"I love you."

"Good. Now be cruel."

A little later, when I awoke again, I saw her standing at the window looking out at the night. "I thought you were cold," I said.

She turned to me and smiled. "You must have been dreaming."

"I may still be. You are here, aren't you?"

"I'm here. Ask me why because you'll like the answer."

"Why?"

"Because I couldn't keep away. Because last night at the Plaza . . . at the Plaza, mind you . . . it was very bad without you. It was like withdrawal pains. How's that?"

"Come back to bed."

She did and I folded her close, her head in my neck and my face in her hair. I breathed in deeply to get all the clean, lovely smell of her. "Lots of bright stars," she said. "No rain tomorrow."

"I could have told you that without looking."

"How?"

"No aches in the old bones."

"Watch that."

"Watch what?"

"How you talk about those bones of yours. I happen to be extremely fond of each and every one of those bones. How many bones are there, incidentally?"

"Seventy-three."

"Seventy-three bones in the human body?"

"Exactly."

"Are you sure?"

"How many did you think there were?"

"Seventy-one."

"There are exactly seventy-two bones in the human body."

"Solomon," she said, giggling. "My own dear sweet Solomon. What time is it, Sol?"

I looked at my watch and the glowing numbers informed me it was ten past twelve. I reported this to her. "I better be going, hadn't I?" she said.

"Why?"

"So you can get your sleep. You always want your sleep before a big match. I shouldn't have come here at all tonight. I know that, but I felt wicked."

"How do you feel now?"

"You used to say it was harmful to make love the night before a big match."

"I used to say a lot of stupid things."

"It isn't harmful?"

"Why do you ask?"

"Just idle curiosity."

"I hate idleness."

"Wait a minute. Wait a minute now. What time is your match tomorrow?"

"The shank of the day, for God's sake."

"The what of the day?"

"The shank, the shank."

"Wait. Just this one more thing."

"Meg . . ."

"No, really, it's important. It's what I came here to say. I don't care if you play tennis until you're a hundred, you're not getting rid of me. There. Was it important?"

"Yes."

"I told you."

"I don't know what to say."

"You're not supposed to say anything. But now you can do

some things if you want to." She took my hands. "Like this and like this."

"Meg, I'll be better to you this time."

"Well, maybe you will, and maybe you won't."

"I promise."

"Promises, promises."

"Meg, please believe it."

"*Make* me," she said fiercely.

And still later: "How do you feel about bra-lessness?" she asked.

"Politically or aesthetically?"

"For me."

I gave this thought. "For you, I think it would be fine. How do you feel about bra-lessness?"

"I think I might go that way."

"Good."

"Why are you smiling?"

"What else would you like my views on?"

"I just happened to be thinking about bra-lessness. I mean bra-lessness popped into my mind so I thought I'd ask you about it. You used to be stuffy about things like that."

"Was I?"

"Very."

"Well, I told you I've changed."

"Have you changed about babies, too?"

"Yes."

"I'm glad. I was going to have some—"

"Some?"

"One to start with. I was going to have one anyway, but I'm glad you won't mind."

"You were going to have one whether I minded or not?"

"Yes. I know that sounds dreadful, but it was the deal I made with myself at the Plaza. Tennis for babies. I won't lie to you."

"Tennis for babies. It sounds like a slogan. Bundles for Britain. Americans for Democratic Action."

"You *don't* mind, do you?"

"No. I like the idea."

"If it's a boy, you can teach him to play tennis. I've thought about it and decided it's all right."

"And if it's a girl?"

"You can try, but she'll probably inherit her mother's net game."

"Tell me something."

"What?"

"What were you thinking about when you started this discussion—babies or bra-lessness?"

"Both."

I tried to make love to her again, but she wouldn't permit it. She wriggled her small, smooth body free of me and skipped it out of my bed. I don't remember anything else. Sleep fell on me like a wall.

CHAPTER 6

FINALS

It is nice to awakened by a kiss on the eyes. *And* breakfast in bed. Meg was responsible for both, and then when she saw I was stirring she drew the curtain to let the sun, warm and brilliant, slosh into the room.

"A day for winners," she said, smiling. She wore a white tennis dress, and she looked lovely in it. Healthy and lovely, brown and golden, the sun playing golden games with her silky hair. "It's half-past nine, sluggard. Eat your breakfast, and then I'll hit lobs to you so you can work the kinks out of your overhead."

"Come here first," I said, patting the bed.

"No."

"Why not?"

"Because you're so easily distracted."

"Just one good morning kiss."

"You've already had it. For your information, Timmy's at Forest Hills sharpening up for you."

"He is?"

"Well, on his way at least. Berto drove him there. Which reminds me." She handed me a piece of notepaper. "From Berto," she said.

Once again, the familiar typescript: "Knock 'em dead, *compadre*. Carbon copy to Timmy."

I grinned. "Did you read it?"

"He showed it to me. He said if you wanted to make something out of getting the original, that was up to you. Come on now, eat your eggs. In protein, there is strength."

Meg had been a lobbing machine for half an hour or so when I became aware of an onlooker seated in the grass behind me—Horowitz, sweaty in a dark suit much too heavy for the weather. For another ten minutes I ignored his presence. He was very good about it. He kept respectfully silent. But when I signaled to Meg that the practice session was over, he got up at once so that he could meet us coming off the court. "She helps you good," he said.

"Yes."

"How's Mrs. Cooper?"

"She's fine," Meg said. "I spoke to her this morning. Doctor says she can go home tomorrow."

"Wonderful, wonderful. Glad to hear it." He turned to me. "Good luck today, Mr. Mathews."

"Thanks. Did you wish Timmy good luck?"

"As a matter of fact, I did."

"Before or after you asked him if he wrote that note to Ann?"

"A cop's head he's got," he said to Meg. "Suspicious."

"But in a nice way."

He kept looking at her. Then, astonishing me, he said, "Listen, my grandfather used to say with age comes wisdom sometimes. Sometimes, he used to say. Not always, mind you, but sometimes. It happens. Maybe it'll happen to him."

"Maybe what will happen to me?"

"Wisdom."

"You're not coming in clear, Horowitz."

"You two are lovey-dovey again, ain't you?"

He waited a moment for one of us to speak. Neither of us did. "I'm a demon," he said, rolling his eyes. "Ask Mr. Farragut. He'll tell you." He started away from us, but after a few feet he stopped. "You should live and be well," he called back, and then, laughing, he took his not so stately girth out of sight.

"What was his evidence?" I said. "Watching us play tennis? That's ridiculous."

"Maybe he *is* a demon?"

"Did you talk to him at all this morning?"

"Just pleasantries. He spent most of his time with Wally."

"Wally?"

"Timmy a little. But mostly with Wally."

I kept silent a moment, thinking.

"Maybe it was body language or something like that," Meg said. "I'm serious. That's possible, isn't it?"

"I suppose so."

"Anyway, is it important?"

"No."

"So why are you looking so somber?"

"I'm wondering now what he was doing with Wally."

"The note?"

"I don't know." Then, in disgust, I added, "That Horowitz. There isn't an inch of him that isn't devious."

Suddenly, her hand went to her mouth. "Goodness me, I almost forgot to tell you."

"What?"

"This is really a dreadful house, you know. Yes, it is. Everybody jumping in and out of bed with everybody else. When I left your room last night, guess whose den was being sneaked into."

"Wally's?"

"He was the sneaker. Who was the sneakee?"

"Ann."

She nodded, watching. "It doesn't upset you? Not the least little bit?"

"I view it as the price Wally has to pay for being filthy rich."

"Are you sure it doesn't upset you?"

"On the other hand, maybe she'll be good for him. The one predictable thing about Ann is she's unpredictable."

"Are you absolutely sure?"

"Don't be an idiot. Of course I am."

"Then you may kiss me."

I did. After which she said, "She's not so unpredictable. I'm as unpredictable as she is."

"Right."

"You didn't predict me sneaking into *your* bed, did you?"

"Never."

"Poor Magruder. Nobody sneaks into her bed."

"Where is she anyway? At the club?"

"Yes. She wanted Wally to drive her, but he wouldn't. He said he had to wait for Ann, and Ann is still asleep. But that's predictable, isn't it? I imagine she goes at things . . . vigorously?"

It may have been an active question, but I decided, silently, to regard it as rhetorical. And she allowed me to. "Poor Dot," she said. "Her face fell a foot. She'll skunk Nell Duncan today, and win her grand slam, but I don't know that it will compensate."

"It will compensate."

"There speaks the tennis player."

"It's just that it's hard for me to see Wally outweighing Paris, Wimbledon, Sydney, and Forest Hills."

"Wally? Or anybody?"

"Peace," I said, showing her my palms. "Let's take a swim."

"Do we have time?"

"A fifteen-minute swim. Get your suit and your suntan lotion, and I'll meet you at the pool."

"Why do I need my suntan lotion for a fifteen-minute swim?"

"Fool," I said, kissing the top of her head. "It's a prop."

I was gently caressing the lotion into her back, her sweetly muscled, narrow, vulnerable back—studying it, feeling protec-

tive toward it, and thinking that with breasts and legs getting
the lyrical lion's share down through the years backs had been
defamed by default—when Wally, fully clothed, materialized
at the far end of the pool, dropped heavily into a chaise, and
all but ignored our greetings.

"He looks angry," Meg whispered. "Don't you think so?"

"Yes."

"What else are you thinking?"

"I'm thinking I have fallen hopelessly in love with your
back. The rest of you is okay, but it's your back I adore.
Will your back marry me?"

"I'll ask it."

"When?"

"After the match." She got up on an elbow and turned so
that she could watch me. "Are you going to win today,
Matty?"

"How can I tell?"

"But do you have a feeling going in?"

"More or less."

"What is it?"

"More or less?"

"Yes."

"That I'll lose. And if I do, I've been thinking I'll bow out
anyway, despite what you said to me so beautifully last night."

She sat up now and put her hands to the sides of my face.
"What will that do to you, my dearest, losing?"

"It'll hurt."

"A lot?"

"Enough."

"Then don't lose, Matty. Please don't lose. I don't want
you to lose. I simply won't have it."

I took her hands and brought her to her feet. "A last wet
down," I said.

"Matty . . ."

"Hush," I said. "I've got you back, back and all. And if your back says yes, I'm home free, right?"

"My back says yes."

"Does the rest of you go along?"

"There was never any doubt about the rest of me."

I moved her to the edge of the pool, and we dived in, hands clasped. We swam a fast length, returned, and climbed out. As we did, Meg said, "He looks so grim. Shouldn't we go and talk to him?"

"Wouldn't do any good, I'm thinking."

"Why not?"

"Because, I'm thinking, Horowitz accomplished the thing he came here to do. Whatever that was. And when Horowitz moves, the rest of us become irrelevant."

But Meg is not always an easy girl to convince. "Aren't you going to the matches, Wally?" she asked as we came up to him.

"Later," he said. "Soon as Ann gets up."

On the face of it, responsive. But Wally's face was something else. It was something from a quarry. His glance went through Meg—focused on nothing here.

"Are you all right?"

He waved a hand at her, abruptly dismissing her, and I drew her away, putting my arm around her when she shuddered. "I don't like that," she said. "It scares me."

"Scares you?"

"I think he wants to hurt someone."

Now—Timmy and I loosening up before the match, only I'm not loosening. The sun beats down on me. The collective gaze of fifteen thousand buffs beats down on me. And I don't know which is causing more sweat. Nerves. Those lines from Kipling's "If" . . . emblazoned here as well as at Wimbledon . . . about triumph and disaster being twin impostors which must be treated just the same . . . slither through my mind on little rat feet. They're trapped there. I can't spring the trap. Insane. Nerves, nerves. I hit a forehand ten feet beyond the base line and Timmy stares at me. I hear indrawn breaths from the spectators. I hear everything, everywhere; antennae out in all directions. Wrong, I tell myself. Concentrate, *concentrate*. You're a veteran, you've been champion here. *You're a goddam disgrace.* Then, drowning, I search out Meg in the first row behind Timmy's side of the court. She sees me looking. She thumbs her nose. A blow struck for perspective. I take two deep breaths, the crowd recedes, and suddenly I am seeing the tennis ball. Rhythm. What a marvelously therapeutic thing it is. The mother and father of confidence. Timmy, phlegmatic, has been hitting ropes. He's getting them back now.

Match underway, Timmy serving. Ace. Netted return. Strong return, backhand to backhand, but he reaches mine and I can't his. Ace. Game to Mr. Clark. Just like that. Less than five minutes. Awed buzzing from the buffs.

My serve. Serving well, but Timmy whacking hell out of balls he should be struggling for. Everything hits chalk for him. Service break: two games love. Four games love. I've made one error, *one*, and I'm down four games. Is he a machine? He's not, goddammit. He's human. I dig in. Fifth game. Timmy serving and leading 30–0. I climb back to deuce. Long rally. Timmy hits wide to my backhand, I scramble there somehow, flick it back, take his return on my forehand and send it scorching down the line. His eyes flicker. I grin at him. He double-faults to lose his service.

I win two more games, but the charge is belated. Need another service break to get back in the set. Can't get it. Reach ad in the ninth game, but then I blow an overhead. Timmy braces. Two blistering serves to close it out. His set, 6–3.

But I feel good. Loose, strong, almost cocky. I sense he *is* worried about his backhand. His volleying is sharp, heavily angled, but his backhand makes him feel vulnerable. I plan to work hell out of it.

The next set is classic. The buffs are in ecstacy, waves of love laving us three points out of five. Timmy and I are misers, handouts only at Christmas. Eleven games follow service. In the twelfth, leading 6–5, I earn an ad with a forehand cross-court off a weak second serve. Set point. I crouch, racket twirling, balanced forward, waiting. A thunderbolt, can't reach it, but I see it miss the line. Will the linesman call it? He does. Timmy is stricken. He glares at the linesman. The seventy-five-year-old linesman stares back, unmoved. I want to kiss his weathered cheek. Timmy serves again. Over-cautious now. Spins it to my backhand, but short. I'm all over it, smashing it deep and rushing behind it to reach the net. Timmy's return is a broken-winged bird. Crunch. Putaway. Sets are even.

Adrenalin hypos through me. I am eagle. I am Superman. I can't be beaten. In proof, I double fault three times and still hold service to start the third set. We change courts. I see diamond droplets on Timmy's black brow. But it is *merely* sweat, not dismay. As usual we say nothing to each other. We are lockjawed tennis players, wrapped in cocoons of silence to protect concentration. Everything works for me now. I have every stroke. I can make every shot from every part of the court. I know it. I do it. At the end of six, I lead 4–2 and am going away. Now, do you remember what I told you about tennis? A bitch-goddess. Deuce in the seventh game. My serve, Timmy's return. His ball takes a Forest Hills bounce in mid-court . . . a shocking bounce on a shoddy return, and I net what I should have put away. Ad to him. I try not to think about it, but it captures an edge of my mind. And because it does, I aim rather than hit through my serve. Not enough pace, not nearly deep enough. Timmy blasts it cross-court, his best backhand of the match, and I am five feet from it as it bites into the grass. His game, service breaks are equal.

The buffs murmur. They see it for what it is, a champion's shot. And they know about champions. Let them out of their cages, and they claw you to shreds. They sense a shift. They are right. The seventy-five-year-old linesman calls one in Timmy's favor. I hate the face I loved. I fight Timmy grimly. I give him nothing. What he gets he earns, but he is a wall. I hit at him and everything comes back. Seven-five. He leads two sets to one.

Now I am thinking too much. Before I was hitting freely, daringly. I was a swashbuckler, raiding for winners on every point. Now I am a cautious old general, plotting my tactics in a rear-echelon tent. Worrying about supply lines. Worrying about my capacity to fight a long war. Worrying about my legs. He breaks my service, wins his own easily, and leads 2–0. Four more games to set, match, and championship. And all he need do is hold service.

Inventory time. Do you want this? Come on now, you miserable sluff-off, you dirty old has-been, do you really want it? How badly do you want it? More than he does is the answer gurgling up from some deep, hot cavern. Just short of dying for it. I come roaring back, in a rage for a service break. Not that Timmy wilts. He stiffens, but I am the corsair again, greedy and savage, and I want what I want. Two shots at it fail. Once I lead 15–40, but he holds me off. Tenth game now. From rocky soil, I have again scrabbled break point. Timmy serves. I pound it back. A long base line rally, four exchanges. Off a hard, forcing forehand, he comes in to attack. But my return is treacherous, half-speed, skimming the net. He lunges for the backhand volley, just gets it back. He is off balance, out of position, and I lob him wickedly. He turns to run for it, but there is no hope. Too deep. Top spin bounces it away from him, and as the buffs explode, the little scoreboard behind the boxes keels over histrionically.

Games are 5-all.

Ten minutes later, 6-all.

Sudden Death, the red flag waving, and the gallery bug-eyed and still as snow.

Five mangy points, I tell myself wheedlingly. Five cruddy points, and you take the set and deuce the match. Five out of nine. You get five, he gets the dregs, and there's no way he can stop you after that. Momentum. It'll be working for you. He'll feel it. Five lousy points. That's all. Forget your goddam legs. *Concentrate.*

At the other end of the court, waiting to receive, Timmy seems emotionless. But I know he's not. I know he's doing what I'm doing, juicing himself. Juice against juice. I serve twice, he serves twice, we change courts and repeat. Passing shots, lobs, dinks, cross-court screamers, an ace mixed in, and not one error. And the score's 4–4. The buffs are wild, standing. The umpire must halt the match to restore order. In the interval, sucking for breath, I look at Meg. She does not see me. Her eyes are scrunched shut.

The ultimate point now. My set point, his match point. Either I win the set, or he wins the match, no other options. Only in Sudden Death can one point be so fateful. He tosses. I watch the ball from the moment it leaves his hand. He hits it big to my backhand and races in after it. But I return with firmness, harder than he expects, and all he can do is half volley weakly to the service line. He is mine now. No way he can escape me, and the thrill of this sings in my blood as I close in for the kill. I smash with my forehand . . . twice more with my forehand . . . and the gallery roars its shock because somehow he has stopped the first two and put away the third.

And I am suddenly dead. Just like that, it is all over—6–3, 5–7, 7–5, 7–6, read 'em and weep. Which is what I want to do, bitterly, but I can't. Grown men can't cry with fifteen thousand people watching them. The obligatory smile. He shakes my hand and says, "You battled, man." I nod. Can't trust myself to talk yet. I see Meg biting her lip.

The mayor speaks, the tournament chairman speaks, all the dignitaries say kind things. Timmy is gracious. He blames my defeat on Sudden Death and adds that it is a lousy way to win. I manage to utter something about what a tremendous player he is, which is true, but I don't feel much like saying it yet. Still, I get the words out, and the buffs applaud as hard as if I'd produced them willingly.

We take our trophies and checks and move past the newsman/cameraman/photographer phalanx toward the pressroom for our interviews. Meg hugs me tightly, never mind how sweaty I am. She is doing my thing for me, crying. She releases me. "If you so much as hint you'll retire I'll never speak to you again." I stare at her. She means it, and suddenly I feel a little better. She sees this and works up a grin. Then she snatches the check from me. "You can't retire," she says. "We need a lot more of these for the family I have in mind."

And so a bit under four hours after I left the locker room— as nervy and wound-tight a finalist as ever there was—I approached it again, beaten but already several degrees less desperate about it. Timmy had said it best. I'd battled. Already I was telling myself bracing things like, you'll be back next year. Well, it was true. And maybe . . . just maybe . . . I'd be luckier.

Berto, waiting at the entrance, put his arm about my shoulders and walked in with me. "Heroic," he said. "So beautiful a match they will be lying about it for centuries. A proud defeat, *compadre*. You feel that yourself?"

"A little."

"Again and louder."

"Yes," I said.

He examined me carefully. "That's better," he said.

Timmy was inside and some other tennis types as well, but newsmen and crowd types were being kept away by Forest Hills security. "I still don't believe those three volleys," I said to Timmy.

He grinned. "Self-defense. I see tracer bullets coming at my middle, and if I don't get the racket up I'm crippled for life. Man, you left me no choice."

"I left you a choice, all right."

"Like what?"

"You could have fainted."

He laughed. Winners laugh easily. He was still laughing when all hell broke loose in the West Side Tennis Club locker room. Wally, screaming, came charging in. Lumbering after him, I saw Horowitz and a uniformed cop. In the confusion I didn't understand what Wally was screaming, thinking, in that first crazy moment, that it was some kind of battle cry. It was, I suppose. "Animal, animal," is what he was chanting over and over again as he leaped on Timmy and hit him with a punch that began at his ankles. While we watched, frozen, Timmy, arms outflung, performed a series of improvised ballet steps climaxing in a pirouette at the far wall. He sat down hard at the base of it. Blood gushed from his nose.

Wally stood over him. "I'll kill you, I'll kill you. Go near her ever again, and I'll kill you." His hands were curved into claws. His voice was a screech. And though you couldn't see the white eye-holed sheet, you knew it was there.

Then, as one, we all started forward, but Horowitz got to Timmy first. The uniformed cop grabbed Wally—who was back to chorusing animal—and pinioned his arms behind him.

"Sorry about this, Mr. Clark," Horowitz said, dabbing at Timmy's nose with a handkerchief. "We tried to stop him outside, but he broke right by us. You all right?"

"Yes."

By this time Berto and I were aiding Timmy to his feet. "You're sure you're all right?" I asked.

"Yes," he said again. But then, as if suddenly realizing what had happened, he tried to tear free of us. We held on for dear life as Horowitz shouted, "Nolan, take Mr. Edmiston for a walk." Nolan, the uniformed cop, with help from two of the onlookers, hurried Wally out of the room.

Horowitz started after them, then stopped. "If you want to prefer charges, Mr. Clark . . ."

"I don't," Timmy said, biting the words off.

"Didn't think so. Little misunderstanding between friends. Little horseplay, no more than that, right?"

"Yes," Timmy said. He was seated on the bench now, head down, staring at the floor.

Horowitz studied him, a look in which I thought I saw more fellow feeling than was usually mirrored in a Horowitz look. But at that moment I didn't know whether this was because of what Wally had done or what Horowitz himself was planning to do.

On the drive back I told Meg about the fight in the locker room, and she went right to the heart of the matter. "And you think Horowitz rigged it?"

"It's like him."

"Why would he do it?"

"I don't know, but it has all the earmarks of a Horowitz gambit. A trap of some kind, with Timmy as fall guy. I mean Horowitz was so conveniently *there* . . . right behind Wally. But just not close enough to stop him in time. I'd lay three to one he tailed Wally from Elinore's and had him staked out until the moment he came busting into the locker room. He must have wanted Wally to slug Timmy. And this morning, that's what he must have been working on . . . prodding him with stuff about Timmy and Ann."

"Didn't Wally know about Timmy and Ann?"

"Probably. I mean Wally's not the most discerning man who ever lived, and he could have missed it if Ann really wanted him to. But even if he did, it's my guess she told him about it . . . in her own way, of course, just so there wouldn't be any surprises. So there's Wally knowing and trying to follow Ann's outline . . . however she put it to him. And there's Horowitz operating on him because for some cockeyed reason he wants Wally to slug Timmy."

"Cockeyed?"

"You're right. I take that back. Whatever the reason is, it makes sense in Horowitz's terms. It's just that I probably wouldn't like it much."

She looked at me. "Funny," she said.

"What is?"

"I thought you kind of dug Horowitz."

"He's the complete hunter. The only thing he really gives a damn about is prey. But he's honest about that, so it does make him hard to hate."

She smiled.

"Why?" I asked.

"You sound so certain."

I nodded. "I know what you mean. You mean there's hunter in me, too. It's in the way I play tennis."

"I used to think so. You know what I thought today?"

"Tell me."

"You'll laugh."

"Tell me anyway."

"Lancelot and Galahad. Galahad, that was Timmy. Faultless and pure and very hard. And Lancelot . . ."

"Not so pure."

"But very human. And brave, and so gallant. I told you you'd laugh."

"I'm not laughing."

"I know it doesn't really fit, but it's what I thought. And I loved you for being Lancelot."

"And losing?"

"But you lost so beautifully. Now you *are* laughing."

"Yes."

"Why?"

"Sit closer to me."

She did and slipped her arm around my waist. "I'm laughing," I said, "because it's so strange to lose and feel like a winner."

"Ah, Matty, that was nice."

We drove in silence for a while and then she said, "Are you hungry?"

"No."

"Tired?"

"A little."

"Oh."

"A little, I said."

"What are we going to do when we get back to the house?"

"We're going to take our ease, as the expression goes. And then we're going to get ready for the big victory party on the roof of the big, plush hotel, where we'll have a big time for ourselves as the next-to guests of honor."

"That's not until nine o'clock. What are we going to do while we're taking our ease."

I leered at her.

Meg had gone back to her room to dress for the party, and I was just thinking about getting out of bed to do the same when the knock came at the door. It was Berto. "The lieutenant just drove up," he said. "I saw him from my window."

"So? On red letter days, the lieutenant does *not* drive up."

"I think he wants to speak to me, *compadre*. I have that feeling. Do you mind if he speaks to me here? In effect, it will be the explanation I promised you."

I swung my feet out of bed, so that I could see him better, so that I could study his face. There was something in his tone that made me nervous.

"Have you forgotten I promised you an explanation?"

"Of course I haven't forgotten. But what's Horowitz got to do with that?"

"Patience, *compadre*. Just a little longer now." He sat down

in a chair, crossed one leg over the other, and leaned back
to wait. He looked impassive, suddenly very Spanish. A few
minutes later we heard Horowitz's size twelves in the corridor. Berto had left my door ajar, and Horowitz stuck his head
in the opening. No smile. Horowitz's face without a smile . . .

"Mr. Ramirez," he said, ignoring me.

"Come in, lieutenant."

"I'd like to talk to you, Mr. Ramirez," Horowitz said,
remaining in the doorway.

"I understand that."

"Alone."

"Not necessary."

"I think it is."

"Well, then, you are wrong."

Horowitz looked thoughtful, then shrugged and shut the
door behind him. He took the other chair. "Mr. Clark's blood
type is A," he said at once. And as he did, I saw him dabbing
at Timmy's nose with his handkerchief and knew why he
had staged that scene.

"Same as Mr. Edmiston's. Blood brothers kind of," he
added, smiling thinly. "Normal. As normal as Mr. Mathews's
blood type, which is B. Or Miss Fraser's, which is B. Miss
Cronin and Miss Magruder are A's. All very normal. Not
even an AB or an O to shake things up a little. We checked
their types after they gave blood for Mrs. Cooper, who happens to be an A. Now two of you didn't give blood, so two
of you—to my way of thinking—might have had something
to hide. After this afternoon's fracas we could check Mr.
Clark's blood type, so we know it wasn't him, right? I mean
stop me any time you want to, Mr. Ramirez."

Berto kept silent. He looked interested but dispassionate.
He looked like a judge sifting evidence in order to render
the most impeccable of verdicts.

Horowitz continued. "Our first problem was the nudity.
A bum steer, as it turned out, but then maybe we shouldn't

blame ourselves too much. I mean nudity, by definition, *is* sexual, right? And there *was* the fact that Mr. Cooper had sex minutes before he was killed, so maybe we can let ourselves off the hook a little for going down the first garden path we came to. It looked inviting as hell, that path. You see, I kept asking myself the wrong questions. I kept asking myself things like—what is the killer trying to *say* by leaving Mr. Cooper naked. Instead of asking myself what is the killer trying to *finesse* by hiding—or, as the case probably was, burning—Mr. Cooper's clothes. Bloodstains, sure. I know that now. But I'd been thinking wrong about blood. I'd been thinking only about Mr. Cooper's blood. It wasn't until all but two of you became donors that I began to think right about blood. The killer *did* have bloodstains to conceal. His own, Mr. Ramirez, his own." He waited, Berto said nothing—nor did I, though by this time my stomach had begun tying itself in knots—and Horowitz went on.

"When the killer struck Mr. Cooper with the lamp, he must have got hit himself by recoil. I mean by that, Mr. Cooper's head must have banged his nose or his mouth, maybe, hard enough to draw blood and leave a stain on Mr. Cooper's clothes. Not the killer's clothes, *Mr. Cooper's clothes*. Not a lot of blood, just one small stain maybe. One small, interesting stain. Now what would make it interesting? I mean it wouldn't be plain old A or B, now would it?" He paused. He looked at Berto, then he looked at me. "Ask him, why don't you? Ask your friend what we'd find if he let us check out his blood."

"Ask him yourself."

"You would find leukemia," Berto said, matter of factly.

I'd seen it coming. All the signals were there because it made a cohesion of so much that had been floating loose before. But the word itself . . . the word itself. "*Christ!*" I said.

Berto got up from his chair and sat down next to me on the

bed. He put his hand on my chin and wrenched my face toward him. "No nonsense," he said fiercely. "If Berto can go without gloom, his friends can, too. Understood? That must be understood."

"How long have you had it?"

"About two years."

"How long will you . . . ?"

"How long will I live? Six months. Maybe more, maybe less. None of the doctors have chosen to be more specific than that. What matters is that I am in remission now and feel not bad, not bad at all. That is what matters, *compadre,* am I right?"

"Yes," I said.

"I will never have to tell you this again?"

"No."

He released me but kept his eyes on mine. "I know all you wish to say. I know it. Between us, there is no need for words. Words are for strangers." He held my gaze an instant longer, driving this message home, and then his expression changed. It became, of all incredible things, sympathetic. Wordlessly —because words were for strangers—he told me that my pain was new, while his was old and bearable. When he saw that I had accepted this, he returned at once to Horowitz. "Do you have more to add?" he asked.

Horowitz, poker-faced, said, "There's this," and handed him the famous note. I recognized it instantly, but Berto didn't even bother to look at it.

"There is this? What is this?"

"It's a love letter to Miss Cronin. Both it and the threatening letters to Mr. Cooper were written on the same typewriter . . . *your* typewriter."

"*My* typewriter is a sort of family typewriter. On tours, many people use it."

"Did you write this note, Mr. Ramirez?"

Now Berto picked it up and looked at it cursorily. "It seems not. In fact, from the last sentence, it seems clear the writer is talking about me. 'Berto sends his love.'"

Horowitz smiled. "Very good, Mr. Ramirez. Except that you have a way of referring to yourself in the third person from time to time. As, for instance, 'If Berto can go without gloom, his friends can, too.'"

And when he said this, that rankling something that had been lodged in my subconscious moved up and out. Yes, that was what had bothered me about the note. I knew Horowitz was right.

"That is observant of you, Lieutenant," Berto said.

"You did write the note, didn't you?"

Berto glanced around him. "A court of law? This does not appear to be a court of law. And my rights? Am I not to be informed of my constitutional rights?"

"No, no, no," Horowitz said, raising horrified hands. "Just an informal discussion. Nothing more, mind you. Nothing more. It's just that I'm curious about a few things."

"I see. Merely curious."

"Yes. You *were* in love with her, weren't you?"

Berto shrugged. "It seems everyone was at one time or another." He glanced at me. "I am sorry, *compadre*. I was less than truthful with you, but I was ashamed, you see, and the habit of silence had grown on me."

"Ashamed of what?"

"Of having been in love with a whore. I, Berto Ramirez, descended from grandees, in love with a whore . . . ?" He smiled dryly. "It did not sit comfortably with my self-image."

"Is Ann a whore?"

"Isn't she?"

"Yes, I suppose so, technically. Though it's a jolt to have to think of her that way."

"Well, a great whore then. A courtesan. The tennis pro's paramour. How is that?"

"You sound bitter," Horowitz said.

"No," he said emphatically. "If anything I am ashamed of being ashamed. If she is a whore, she is an honest one. She never lied to me, never promised more than she gave. It would make a good epitaph. I would like it for mine. Will you remember, *compadre?*"

"Yes."

"I am serious."

"I'll remember."

He turned to Horowitz again. "Very well, I was in love with her. But that was two years ago. Ancient history."

"Ancient history? So what's ancient history? It's the grandpa of current events."

"Tell me about that, Lieutenant."

"All right, I will. You say it's ancient history, so I say maybe Miss Cronin *didn't* go to the shack to meet you. On the other hand, maybe she did and you're being less than truthful again. Not very important anyway. So let's say you were there by accident. The important thing is you *were* there, right?"

"I am listening."

"But, Mr. Cooper, he was there first. And so you came in on them just after, right? And they were lying there . . . and maybe Miss Cronin, seeing you, screamed—he made me, he forced me, or something like that, right? And so you picked up the lamp, and maybe you hit him harder than you meant to. Or maybe you hit him exactly as hard as you meant to because even in that split second a couple of things might have been in your mind."

"What things, Lieutenant?"

"Related things. One, Cole Cooper is like maybe the world's supreme bastard and doesn't deserve to live. Two, who's in a better position to rid the world of a bastard like that than somebody already sentenced to die. I mean by that leukemia, Mr. Ramirez."

"Of course."

"Are you still listening, Mr. Ramirez?"

"I am still listening. I am waiting to hear what Ann was doing all that time."

"She either watched or ran away. She says Mr. Cooper was alive when she left, but she could be lying. That doesn't matter either. What matters is she knows you were there."

"Has she said so?"

"No," Horowitz said after a moment.

"That is too bad."

Horowitz kept silent.

"Isn't it too bad, Lieutenant?"

"Yes, it's too bad. But it may not be permanent. I wouldn't absolutely count on it being permanent."

"Oh, I think one might. We all know Ann, do we not? She very seldom does a thing from which there is nothing to gain. Particularly if the thing meant involvement in the kind of scandal that might make it even more difficult than it will be for Wally to explain her to his parents. And also she has affection for me. I do not say she would never hurt me. Nothing so sweeping as that. I am not a fool. I do say she would not hurt me unless she thought she had to."

"Sounds to me as if you're admitting something, Mr. Ramirez."

"I admit nothing, Lieutenant. I merely want to make certain things clear for the sake of positioning."

"Positioning?"

"Your position versus mine . . . hypothetically. Will you permit me?"

"Sure."

"Hypothetically now, let us assume for a moment that I am your man. What good is that if you have no case against me? An empty victory."

"Go on."

"And you have no case, no case at all, without Ann to cor-

roborate my presence on the scene. I see a courtroom. I see
this handsome, slightly wan young man sitting there. On his
face, a faint, brave smile, reflecting the nobility of suffering. I
see his clever lawyer underscoring this for the jury. Leukemia,
he says in a hushed whisper. I see the ladies on the jury . . .
there *will* be ladies . . . remembering their sons and lovers.
And I see your case, what case you have, collapsing from sheer
insubstantiality. And so, if you are ready now, I have a deal to
speak of."

"A deal?"

"If you are ready for it. Only if you are ready for it. No
hurry. Take your time and reflect."

"I'm ready," Horowitz said, and in his voice there was the
suspicion of a sigh.

"My words carried weight? You see that courtroom as I
have pictured it?"

"I'm ready, Mr. Ramirez."

"Of course you are. I knew you would be. Actually, you
were ready before you ever came in here, were you not?"

"You're the dealer," Horowitz said. "Me, I'm waiting to
look at the cards."

Berto paused. He narrowed his eyes thoughtfully. He got
up from the bed, returned to his chair where he leaned back
comfortably, crossing his legs while he clasped his hands behind his neck. He said, "Well, then, here they are. I have a
relatively few months to live, and I do not wish to spend that
time being worried at. I do not wish to be the fox to your
hound. You would gain nothing from this. It would be an exercise in futility. You have nowhere to go but up blind alleys.
Still, though you would gain nothing, I would lose. I grant
you that. Do I make myself clear? I want peace. In return I
offer you a confession."

"A confession of what?"

"Of all you desire," Berto said carefully. "A detailed
confession, freely given—and so stated—which I will write out

166

tomorrow and which you will have the opportunity to examine. Upon your approval I will then give it into Matty's keeping until the day after my death. Or, as soon after my death as he becomes aware of it. He will then be honor-bound . . . honor-bound . . . to put it in your hands for whatever use you may wish to make of it." He turned to me. "Matty . . . ?"

I nodded glumly.

"Lieutenant . . . ?"

"Will the confession be along the lines I've been discussing?"

"Close enough," Berto said, smiling. "You reconstruct neatly. You should be pleased with yourself."

Horowitz looked far from pleased.

"You'll get your man," Berto said. "A little later than you would like, but that can't be helped, can it? And perhaps the victory will be all the sweeter for the wait. Well?"

But Horowitz was still in a mood to temporize. "*Did* you go to the shack to meet her?"

"It will be in the confession."

"The hell with the confession. Answer the goddam question."

"Very well, the answer is yes."

"Why?"

"She asked me to."

"Why?"

"She said she was having backhand problems and wanted me to help her," Berto said blandly.

"I don't believe that."

"Perhaps I didn't either."

"It wasn't a backhand lesson she wanted from you."

"Perhaps I thought not also."

"And you were willing?"

Berto shrugged. "Why not? Consider my life expectancy, Lieutenant."

"And when you swung the lamp, were you considering your life expectancy then, too?"

Berto took a moment before replying. "I have thought about that," he said. "Perhaps murder *was* in my mind at that moment. I am not certain. What is certain is that I do not regret what I did. He was, as you say, a supreme bastard."

"That doesn't justify murder."

Berto stiffened. His voice was icy. "I do not ask *you* for justification. I ask *you* only for an answer to my proposition."

Horowitz turned to me. "He's a beaut, ain't he? And this is sure as hell a pretty kettle of fish."

"Do it, Horowitz," I said. "For Christ's sake, say yes and get it over with."

He turned back to Berto. "What with new drugs and everything, I've heard it said leukemia patients can live as much as ten years."

"I assure you that is not the case here."

Horowitz got up and went over to the window. He stood there for a long moment, staring out. "You know, not one person in my entire family wanted me to be a cop. Why? Because they hate cops? No. Because they knew I'd make a lousy one. My mother . . . do I have to tell you what my mother wanted me to be? A doctor, right. My grandfather said, Jacob, you like your own way too much to be successful at it, and they will make you suffer for this. My brother wanted me to go into the dress business with him. It's a good business. There's a living in it. Is there a living in being a cop? *Such* a living. My wife said cops shmops and walked out on me. But my father, maybe he said it best. You're a bandit yourself, he said. Well, the hell with 'em all. The hell with 'em all, I say." The monologue ended, he slowly levered himself around so that he was facing me. "He *was* a Hitler, wasn't he?"

"I think so."

"And you, you know what you're making yourself? An accessory after the fact."

"All right."

"And I'm a shmuck," he said, and then tilted his head toward Berto. "Your pot."

"Does that mean we have an arrangement?"

"Yes," Horowitz said. He plopped himself into his chair and fastened a gaze full of *Weltschmerz* to the ceiling.

"I will visit you tomorrow afternoon," Berto said.

"No," Horowitz said, not moving his eyes. "You will call me, and I will visit you."

Berto nodded. To me, he said, "By and by, *compadre*."

"Where are you going?"

"To get ready for the party, of course. With Matty and Timmy as guests of honor, did you imagine that . . ." He stopped deliberately and glanced at Horowitz. "Did you imagine that *Berto* would not be there to drink your health?" A moment later he was gone.

"Cool, isn't he?" Horowitz said.

"Yes."

"I'm not sure I like him. Not at all sure he isn't just another cold-blooded murderer. But that's irrelevant, isn't it? What's relevant is how *you* feel about him. And you'd lie to hell and gone for him, wouldn't you?"

"Yes."

"And Miss Cronin, too. Well, maybe not to hell and gone, but just as he said."

"Don't let it bug you, Horowitz. You were in a box. You got the best deal you could have. Your chief of police couldn't have done better."

"The hell with him, too. That's not what bugs me."

"What bugs you?"

"Seeing him walking out of here grinning. It goes against the grain to have him beat me."

"Now that's funny. That really is funny."

"Why is it funny?"

"Horowitz, Horowitz, he's got leukemia."

"Yeah," he said after a long moment, "there is that, ain't there?" He stood up. "I guess you'll be in contact."

"You heard him. I'm honor-bound."

He stood there—huge, shaggy, and dispirited—staring at his shoe tops as if there were a lesson to be derived from them. "You know, in a lot of ways this was the worst case I was ever on," he said. "Very little satisfaction. Almost no satisfaction at all. But I did learn one thing."

"What?"

"About tennis players."

"What?"

"By and large, they ain't no dumber than cops."

He held out his hand, and I took it. Both of us self-conscious, but we got it done. Then, like a locomotive in search of lost minutes, he chugged from the room. A few seconds later I followed him out. I had to find Meg. I needed her badly.

CHAPTER 7

POST MORTEM

We were at Hurlingham, which is the Victorian sporting club where tennis people gather in the fortnight before Wimbledon, when we got the word that Berto was dead. Timmy brought it to us—a letter from Berto's father. It was a brief letter, written after the funeral. Those had been Berto's instructions, none of us to be notified until *after* the funeral. Two months earlier, when he had said his good-bys to us, he had told us he wanted it that way. Then he had gone home to die. Peacefully, the letter said. I hoped it was true. I passed the letter to Meg. She read it and returned it to Timmy.

For a long while we sat in silence under one of the giant copper beeches, sipping Pimm's Cups and looking out at the expanse of barbered lawns—tennis lawns, croquet lawns, bowling lawns—and the array of genteel people putting them all to use. It was an aspect exceedingly civilized and teeming with Englishness. "Berto always loved it here," Timmy said finally.

"And they loved him here," I said. "Though he liked to shake them up a little. I remember once when they served his tea, and he asked . . . oh, very politely . . . if it would be possible to substitute tortillas for the strawberry tart."

"Man, it's hard to get used to," Timmy said softly. "I keep thinking it's like we're playing in different tournaments, that's all. And that when this one's over, he'll turn up at the next. But he won't, will he?"

"No."

He looked at me. "Could you have done what he did? Killed Cole, I mean?"

"Did he do it intentionally? Elinore swears it was an accident."

"That's Elinore."

"Yes, I suppose so."

"Berto told me that the night he had dinner with her in her room . . . the night she cut her wrists . . . he went up there to tell her he was sick. And he did. And then he said he suddenly started to cry. It just grabbed him . . . the whole thing . . . and before he knew it he was crying and she was holding him and rocking him back and forth." He paused and shook his head. "Berto crying," he said.

I kept silent. I felt Meg's hand tighten on mine.

"So he told her. I mean about Cole. He hadn't intended to, but he did. And she said he couldn't have meant to kill Cole. Why? Simple. Because she knew Berto wasn't a killer. Therefore, it had to have been an accident."

"Which she could forgive."

"Yes."

"And then she cut her wrists."

He nodded. "You're right," he said. "It wasn't the first time Elinore punished herself for something somebody else did."

"That's the way she is," Meg said. "Would you really have her any different?"

"At least a little," I said.

But Timmy was watching me. "I think she was wrong about it being an accident, do you?"

"Yes."

"*Could* you have done what he did?"

"He asked me that once. It was right after that shoot-out Cole staged, that thing that started with Magruder and ended with everybody shedding blood. Berto asked me, could you kill a man like that?"

"What did you say?"

"I said I might. But at the time I didn't take it as a serious question. I mean I didn't think he meant murder. That is, literally."

"Murder?"

"Wasn't it?"

"Man, the worst I'd ever call it is an execution."

I shrugged and kept silent.

"Well?"

"No," I said. "I don't think I could have done it."

"I could have."

I studied him. "You said that so easily I wonder if Berto would have believed you."

And then, surprising me, he grinned. A moment later the grin had faded. "I miss him like hell," he said bitterly.

Meg, who'd held on to my hand, took it now and rubbed it over her stomach. It was nicely rounded. Watermelon size. Death and life, she was saying to me.

"When's Elinore coming?" I asked Timmy.

"Tomorrow. I pick her up at the airport around ten-thirty."

"Too bad."

"Too bad?"

"She won't enjoy seeing me take you straight sets."

"Dreamer," Meg said.

"Whose side are you on?"

"Your side, man," Timmy said. "But the girl's a realist."

"He'll beat you all right," Meg said. "After all, Timmy, he is better than you are. He's just not quite good enough to take you straight sets."

He laughed. "I better split while I still got some confidence."

"Timmy," I said as he got to his feet.

"What?"

"Wally called last night. He and Ann are coming over for the second week."

"So?"

"I just thought you ought to know."

"Who gives a goddam," he said fiercely, compensating in sound for what he lacked in conviction. He reminded me of someone else I'd once known—me trying to dismiss Meg.

"I feel so sorry for him," Meg said after he was gone.

"Don't," I said. "He'll probably win the championship."

"Big deal, the championship."

"It isn't?"

"You'd trade me for it, child and all, wouldn't you?"

I hesitated.

"Oh, you monster," she said, and almost capsized my Pimm's Cup while raiding my rib cage.

That night we got a wire from Horowitz:

> WHAT THE HELL STOP TEAR IT UP STOP
> LIVE AND BE WELL STOP

N